NAWAB

Omi Singh

Invincible Publishers

First published in India in 2019

ISBN: 978-93-88333-54-2

Invincible Publishers

Registered Address: 201A, SAS Tower, Sector 38, Gurgaon 122003

Dedicated to all my loved One's, family, friends who encouraged and inspired me to conceptualize the idea of "Nawab" and complete the Novel .

Acknowledgements

My proof reader, typist, designer, editor, printer and Publishers

During the pre-Independence era, a twelve year old orphan boy in KalekiMandi, Sialkot (now in Pakistan), earned his livelihood by selling newspapers.He dreamt of becoming a film actor which compelled him to run away from Sialkot and pass through Jammu during the time of partition to reach the dream city, Bombay (now Mumbai).

As fate would have it, Ghulam Mohammad Khan - the same boy who had run awayfrom Sialkot, arrived in Delhi en route to Mumbai, and fell in love with a local girl named Afsha.The by-lanes of Chandni Chowk around the Red Fort in GailKhajanchiin old Delhi became his home.

As time passed, Ghulam Mohammad Khan established his *ittr* business in the vicinity of Fatehpuri Masjid. That twelve year old boy from Sialkot had now grown up to become a man with a decent living with his wife, Afsha Begumand, and a son, Nawab Ghulam Mohammad Khan who took birth on 05th June, 1955.

Nawab Khan spent all his childhood in Chandni Chowk and graduated in Commerce from Delhi University in the year 1974. By the time Nawab completed his graduation, both his parents had passed away. Nawab was a well-built six foot tall handsome boy for whom many girls from the university had developed a liking, but Nawab wasn't interested in them. He was, in fact, attracted to a girl named Ashika who lived in his vicinity, but this relationship never materialised.

During the chilly winter of November'74, Nawab decided to leave Delhi as he could no longer successfully uphold his father's *ittr* business. Eventually, he sold his shop and place of residence in Delhi that had been bequeathed to him by his parents, and travelled to Mumbai via Punjab Mail on 25th December, 1974.

When the Punjab Mail reached Mumbai Central station, Nawab Khan got down from the train with all his belongings that he had carried from Delhi.He looked around for a coolie, till one eventually came up to him from one end of the platform and asked, "*Kahan jana hai, sa'ab?"* (Sir, where do you want to go?)

"*Koee rahane ka intezam karoge*?" (Can you arrange for some accommodation for me?) answered Nawab.

The coolie nodded as he picked up his luggage and said, "*Sa'ab, ek Rupaya lunga.Chalo mere peeche.*" (I will take 1 Rupaya, sir. Follow me.)

Nawab followed the coolie who headed towards the famous Nagapada near Bombay Central. Entering the stinking by-lanes of the place with the coolie, Nawab didn't know that his fate had cut him a one way ticket to Nagapada from were the dignified *pathan*, whose roots lay all the way back in Sialkot, Pakistan, and Delhi, would become the flamboyant Don whose abode for now was *Noorani Manjil,*Nagpada.

He started living in a tiny apartment on the first floor of Noorani Manjil. Nagpada was a very unusual place for Nawab to live in, yet he had no option but to adjust with the times. Though the money which he had received from the sale proceeds of his shop and residence in Delhi was enough to take care of his daily needs for some time, he decided to earn.

Nawab would search through job requirements in newspaper classifieds daily and attempt for interviews too. A few months passed and on 11th March, 1975,he went for an interview at 'Verma Memorial Hospital' which was located in Central Mumbai in Parel, just a few kilometers away from Nagpada.He entered the cabin of the hospital's Dean, Dr. Jagmohan Randhawa.**"P**lease be seated,"the Dean said while glancing at some files on his desk.

"Thank you,sir," said Nawab and reluctantly took the chair on the left out of the three placed in front of the Dean's table.He turned to his right and saw the other two chairs empty.

"Good morning, Doctor." Nawab heard a female voice. An elegant girl in a blue sari, blue bangles on both her wrists,a pink bindi on her forehead, pink lipstick,and a white apron on her entered Dr.Randhawa's cabin.

"Very good morning, Amrita.Please take a seat," replied Dr.Randhawa.

She looked at Nawab as she took a chair next to him.

Dr.Randhawa introduced Amrita to Nawab, who was being interviewed for the post of 'Purchase Officer' in the purchase department. He got through the interview process and was asked to join the Verma Memorial Hospital effectively from 16th March, 1975.

"Amrita, just make him understand his job profile," asked Dr.Randhawa while gesturing at Nawab. "Nawab sahab, congratulations! Please understand all the details and your responsibilities from madam," Dr.Randhawa told Nawab with a smile while looking at Amrita.

"Thank you, sir," both Nawab and Amrita said together and left Dr.Randhawa'scabin.The tall and handsome Nawab Khan accompanied Amrita out while she explained each and every detailof his job profile to him. Nawab followed all her instructions obediently.She finally said after some time,"Khan sahab, I hope you have understood everything.You may join form the 16th. In case of any problem, do ask for me. I sit in the third cabin," said Amrita while pointing at her cabin to her right.

"Thank you, Madam ji. I will report on the 16th," replied Nawab and took her leave. While nearing the exit gate, Nawab turned back and saw Amrita still standing there, chatting with another doctor. Suddenly, he felt the need to get some clarification regarding his credentials and went back to Amrita."Madam ji," he asked, "You were to check my original certificates…"

"Leave it. We will check on the 16th," she replied with a smile.

"Thank you, madam," Nawab replied humbly and zoomed off to the Exit gate.

1975 began with Bollywood blockbusters such as Deewar and Andhi. A movie ban was not a new phenomenon, and the film Andhi faced the same fate for its female protagonist.The character was played by the Bengali beauty Suchitra Sen who bore a close resemblance with the then Prime Minister, Indira Gandhi. Maratha Mandir was a prominent cinema hallin Bombay Central then, and adjacent to it was Café Shalimar.

On 13th March, 1975, at 9 AM in the morning, Nawab was occupyinga corner table at the café and orderedfor an omelet and three bread slices. At the counter, the radio was playing a song from the movie Amanush, which was about to get released on 21st March, 1975.

As the tune of '*Dil Aisa Kisi Ne Mera Toda*' reached Nawab's ears, he was mesmerized by Sharmila Tagore, another Bollywood Bengali beauty who ruled the hearts of many youngsters then. Amanush starred the Calcutta superstar Uttam Kumar opposite Sharmila Tagore in the lead.

In the mid-seventies, Mumbai had its own stars rising from various fields of the spectrum, like cricket, Bollywood, politics, and last but not the least, the underworld, or rather the Mumbai underworld.Some stars were on the verge of fading. Rajesh Khanna faded out and Amitabh Bachchan emerged; Tiger Pataudi faded away and Sunil Gavaskar emerged; Krishna Desai's Communist Party Marxist faded awayand Shiv Sena supremo Bala Thakare emerged; and in the underworld, its very own Mastan and Karim Lala faded away and the son of the constable, Kaskar, slowly emerged and went on to form the (in)famousD-company. Nawab, on the other hand, was in his own world, unaware of where this world was about to take him.

"Give a cup of tea as well," ordered Nawab while finishing his omeletand the last slice of bread with it. In another two minutes, the waiter served him tea and Nawab started sipping on itwhile listening to another song that came fleeting to his ears from the radio kept at the cash counter.'*Is Mod Se Jaate hai Kuch Sust Kadam Raste Kuch Tej Kadam Rahe…*'This song had been written by Gulzar for the film Andhi. The music was another classic composition by Pancham, sung by Lata Mangeshkar and Kishore Kumar.

"Please come here," a female voice from the back seat caught his attention. He turned to find a beautiful lady in white *salwar kameez* and yellow dupatta, with slightly curly hair that fell down to her shoulders, ordering a bystander waiter at the café. Nawab was surprised to see that he had noticed her before at the Verma Memorial Hospital the day he was taking a round with Amrita. "Doone thing, get me *Bhurji Pav* and Campa Cola," instructed the lady to the waiter.

Having finished his breakfast, Nawab got up and moved to the cash counter to pay his bill, while still looking, or rather staring, at the same girl.

"Why are you staring at me like that? Haven't you seen a girl in your life before?" she yelled at Nawab.Unmoved, Nawab simply ignored her and went on to pay the bill.

"How much?" he asked the cashier.

"25 paise total, sir" answered the cashier. While staring at the same lady, Nawab paid his due and left the café.

On 16th March, 1975, Nawab reached Verma Memorial Hospital in the morning. Amrita met him in the corridor as they had both entered the hospitaltogether.They also met Dr.Randhawa who graciously welcomed him and said, "Amrita,please complete all the formalities and see that he gets comfortable. Welcome, Nawab, and all the best.You may begin with your work form today."

"Thank you,"replied Nawab.

"Amrita, I am leaving the rest up to you," instructed Dr.Randhawa.

"Yes, sir,"replied Amrita promptly, and they both exited Randhawa's cabin.

In her cabin, she check through all the original credentials of Nawab who had taken a chair across the desk from her. Just then, somebody peeped in and said, "Amrita, where have you been? I have been looking for you for so long."

When Nawab heard this familiar female voice, he turned around to see the same woman whom he had seen just a couple of days ago at café Shalimar. She looked quite elegant dressed in a pink sari with an apron over it.

"Nafisa, dear, just wait for a moment. I am a bit busy," said Amrita, looking at her. "Listen, this is Nawab Khan. He has joined the hospital as the purchase officer from today," she continued, introducing Nafisa to Nawab.

"Hmmm,"Nafisa reacted in a contemplating manner while looking at Nawab.

"Hello, madam," replied Nawab with a wary look.

Nafisa took the chair adjacent to Nawab's and across fromAmrita, and stared at Nawab who was now sitting right beside her. Nawab did not feel comfortable with Nafisa's looks.

"Madam, where is the washroom?" he asked Amrita.

"Out from here, take a right and then a left," answered Amrita.

Ignoring Nafisa's stares, he got up from his chair and turned towards the door. "Madam, I am leaving this file on your table," Nawab said humbly as heplaced a file and a notepad on her desk.

"No problem," Amrita responded.

As soon as Nawab was out of the cabin, Nafisa revealed to Amrita, "I saw this guy two days ago at café Shalimar. He was staring at me and I gave him a piece of my mind too."

"Oh, Nafisa.He is new to the city," responded Amrita.

"Come on, I am not telling lies," said Nafisa, leaning closer towards Amrita. "See, this man is not right," she continued while flicking her hand to the right. In that moment, her hand hit Nawab's notepad which fell down with a thud.

"Look what you've done now. You don't have any patience,"Amrita said to Nafisa, a little irritatedly.

"Let me pick it up. It's not a big deal." As Nafisa was picking up the notepad, she saw something written on it and started reading the first page.

"Nawab ki mohabbat ek anjaan afsaana hai,

Uske kaee diwane hai, par vo tumhara diwana hai.

Ishq me Nawab ko fareb hi mila,

Ab ke shayad us ki aankho me aitbar dekha hai.

Nawab ki fitrat me izhar nahi hai,

Tum dil se dekho

Nawab ko tumse Mohabbat hai."

(Nawab's love is an unknown saga.He has been adored by many, but he is madly in love with you. Nawab was always betrayed in love, but now he can see true love in your eyes. Nawab isn't expressive of his love, but if you look into his eyes, you'll find that he is in love with you.)

"Amrita, this tall and handsome pathan seems to be a writer," Nafisa said, her tone a little loud and taunting, as if making fun of Nawab.

In response, Amrita simply gave her a look and gestured with her eyebrows that Nawab was standing right behind her. Not taking the hint however, Nafisa continued ina loud voice, "You know, that day at café Shalimar, I gave him a piece of my mind when I caught him staring at me. Poor guy just left without much fuss."

"Madam, I wasn't staring atyou," said Nawab.Nafisa turned to find Nawabstanding right behind her. She fumbled for words and acted as if nothing had happened. "Please return my notepad," Nawab said to Nafisa. Amrita looked at both of them.For a second, there was pin drop silence in Amrita's cabin, and then…everybody burst into laughter. Nawab simply smiled and took his seat.

"I will catch you later," Nafisa said to Amrita and left the cabin. In some time, all of Nawab's joining formalities were completed and he began his innings as the Purchase Officer at this hospital.

Every Sunday, men from Nagpada and its vicinity would rush to Naaz saloon to get a haircut. 23rd March, 1975, was one of those Sundays, and Nawab also made his way to the saloon and waited for his turn to get a haircut. It was almost 11AM in the morning and Nawab waited on a chair kept outside the saloon, a newspaper in his hand. Small children were busy playing gully cricket in a lane across the road from the Saloon. Some burkha clad women were buying meat from the butcher who had his shop set up inone corner of the same lane. It was a busy Sunday morning and people were occupied with their regular household chores.

When Nawab's turn came, he got up from his chair to enter the saloon. The barber adjusted the seat for him and asked, "What style do you want,sir? Rishi Kapoor, Sashi Kapoor, or shall I make it into Bachchan style? Vinod Khanna style may also suit you,sir."

"Just cut my hair properly. Keep it medium length," replied Nawab.

"Fine,sir," said the barber and started working. No sooner had he started, a few men,seemingly in their thirties, forcibly entered the saloon and enquired, "Is pathan here?"

"Who pathan?" asked the barber.

"They are the tall ones," replied one of them.

"There is only one tall guyhere and he looks like a pathan as well," replied the barber, pointing at Nawab.

"Oh, yeah!He is the one. Shoot him!" said one of them and they opened fire at Nawab.

There was absolute chaos at the saloon and Nawab was drenched in blood.The goons soon fled away, while thefellow bystanders called for help. Nawab was immediately rushed to the nearby Dr.Awasthi Hospital in a taxi.In the meantime, police entered the crime scene and enquired about the culprits. They suspected that the shootout was most probably planned to eliminate Karim Pathan, a member of the infamous Pathan gang, and Nawab suffered collateral damage due to mistaken identity.

At the hospital, the doctors operated on Nawab to remove the bullets from his unconscious body, while he dreamt about the one girl whom he had fallen for back in Delhi, Chandni Chowk at Fatehpuri Masjid. Nawab's one way love story had never materialised, but he was silently and madly in love with this girl. Her name was *Ashika*.

He was transported back to that day of Eid when he had succeeded in meeting and talking to her after several failed attempts. Ashika was on the stairs that led up to the Fatehpuri Masjid when Nawab took her aside and proposed to her, "Will you marry me?"

"*Nawab ko ibadat aur sajade ke liye*

Khuda ki chowkhat ki jaroorat nahi.

Tere kadamo me vo apana sir jhukata hai.

Ab tum reham karo ya saza do,

Use koyi fark nahi padata hai…"

(Nawab doesn't need a place of worship to pray to the Almighty. He bows down to your feet.It's up to you now to either shower love on him or punish him.)

She replied that it could not happen. Nawab was silent and remained silent thereafter.A heart was broken at a tender age, but his love for Ashika remained the same, as pure as it had always been. Thus, he dreamt of Ashika.

A beautiful girl, Ashika always remained Nawab's passion and love.If there was one person for whom Nawab could do anything, it was his tender-aged beloved girl, Ashika. As the name suggests, Ashika meantlove, and she was indeed Nawab's love,his life, his passion and everything else. When Nawab was struggling between life and death on that hospital bed, Ashika was nowhere near him, but his unconscious mind took him back to the day when Ashika was to leave her maternal house in Chandni Chowk after marriage.

,Nawab entered discreetly into Ashika's room while she was in her bridal attire, thinking perhaps about beginning her new life post marriage. Nawab was in love with her, but could not get her that time. He told her, "*Ashika, mai tumhe takleef dene nahi aaya, bus ye kehane ayaa hu ke tum sochti hogi mera kya rishta hai tumse.Mai kahu jo meri ruh ka Rab se, dil ka dhadkan se, aur rago ka jism se hai,vahirishta hai tumse. Nawab janata hai vo tumhara shauhar nahi ho sakta,lekintumhara hamsafar ho sakta hai. Ye haq Nawab tumse mang nahi raha hai. Usne khud ko ye haq diya hai.*"(Ashika, I haven't come to trouble you.I just wanted to say that you might wonder what relation I have with you. It is the same that my soul has with God, that my heartbeats have with my heart, and that blood has with my body, that is the connection I share with you. Nawab knows that he won't ever be your beloved husband, but he can be your well wisher.He isn't asking for this right from you.In fact, Nawab has sanctioned himself the right to be so for you.)

Such was his love for Ashika. His words brought tears to her eyes, though she didn't know whether Nawab wasright for her or not at that time. "Nawab, this is destiny.God bless you, take good care of yourself," she said.

Nawab looked at her one last time and left the house in tears. A few years later while still in Delhi, Nawab learned from a local friend in Chandni Chowk that Ashika's marriage had fallen apart and that she was all alone, but her whereabouts where still not known to him. Nawab had accepted his fate,unaware that God had a different plan for him and Ashika.

Ashika – Nawab's only dream and beloved was everything to him, so much so that she was always on his mind. Nawab had been a loner and an aloof man all along, but the thought of Ashika would always bring a sparkle in his eyes. Though his love for Ashika in Delhi was only a one-sided emotion,the Almighty had rewritten their fate.Only he knew that on Earth, Nawab and Ashika are meant and made for each other.Perhaps, the Almighty had decided to bring them back together, otherwise it could not have been a mere co-incidence that the samehospital in which Nawab was undergoing treatment, lying on his death-bed and still dreaming about Ashika, was in fact where she was working at that time in the capacity of a Records Manager.However, she didn't know that Nawab was there in the same hospital, in room no. 111, directly above room 011 which was the Records Department of which Ashika was in charge. Sometimes, individuals decide to apart, but the Almighty brings them close once again.Being with each other was their fate, their destiny, on which neither had any control.

A ward boy rushed to room no. 011 and said, "Ashika ma'am, kindly make apatient file for room no. 111 and bring it to Dr. Awasthi. There is a new patient who seems to be very serious. He's got some bullet injuries. Dr.Awasthi is asking for the file."

"Alright," said Ashika and got a patient'shistory file ready for the new patient.Sherushed to room no. 111 and knocked, "Doctor, you called?"

"Yes, Ashika.Please fill in the details of this patient," instructed the doctor, pointing at Nawab. Ashika glanced at the patient, then moved closer to have a clearer look.

"Doctor, I know him.He is from Delhi.His name is N…Nawab. Why is he here?" she asked.

"Bullet injuries, probably. Some gang war shootout."

Oh! But Nawab can never be a gangster. I am sure of this. I knew him back in Delhi.He never even had a minorscuffle with anyone, then how is this possible?" she asked aghast.

"As per the police, it's a case of mistaken identity. The main target was some other pathan, but they shot him."

Ashika was speechless and stunned.She filled in the details of Nawab while looking at him.After completing, she kept the file on the desk near Nawab's bed and told thedoctor, "Sir, I have prepared and kept the file here."

On coming out of room no. 111,she ran to the washroom on the same floor and cried like a small child inside. She looked in the mirror above the wash basin and thought to herself, 'Nawab,perhaps you don't know this, but I realized the value of your love for me much later in life. My life was like hell after marriage and it didn't work. I thought of you everyday and wished that I had accepted your proposal.' She continued crying and pushed herself against the wall next to the line of washbasins. Her hair were scattered over her face and tears streamed down her cheeks.She felt shattered.

Back at the Verma Memorial Hospital, business was as usual but one man was missing from the scene, i.e., Nawab. He hadn't been to workfor two days, but nobody there knew that he was fighting for his life in other hospital just a few kilometers away. Amrita reported his absence to Dr.Randhawa, who only instructed her to find out from the residential address that Nawab had provided in the records,then revert on the same. Many stories started floating aroundregarding Nawab's absence.He virtually became the topic of gossip for many at the hospital, but none knew the truth.The man himself was fighting the battle against death, unaware that the impression of his character was at stake back at the Verma Memorial Hospital due so somemiscreant who believed in floating false stories around.

At Dr. Awasthi's hospital, Ashika was beside Nawab, watching the man who had always loved her.She tried hard to understand him and why he loved her so much. Many thoughts crossed her mind as she asked herself a medley of questions.She wondered whether Nawab still really loved her.She found her situation completely strange. Ashika had always had Nawabin her subconscious mindand knew that he loved her too, but still these questions returned over and over again to plague her mind. From a distance, she could hear the song being played ona transistor radio that a civilian carried along on the footpath adjacent to the hospital.

"...*Ek pyar ka nagama hai,*

Maujo ki rawani hai,

Jindgai aur kuch bhi nahi,

Teri meri kahani hai..."

After a few days, Nawab opened his eyes.It was the beginning of April, 1975.That morning,bright sun rays filtered through the window of the hospital room where Nawab was lying. Ashika stood by the window,a soft silhouette between the sunrays and Nawab.

"Waa...waaa...ter...water," he murmured faintly.

Ashika turnedto fetch a glass of water, then drew closer to him.When Ashika's face came clear to his vision, he couldn't help but stare at her in surprise. From outside the window,strains of the song *'Aankho Hi Aankho Me Ishara Ho Gaya,Baithe Baithe Jeene Ka Sahara Ho Gaya'* came flitting through another loud transistor radio being carried by some pedestrian. Nawab took the glass of water and sipped, while looking deep into Ashika's eyes.

"Doctor,*pata pada hai Nawab pe goliya chali thee beete dino*," Amrita informed Dr. Randhawa. (I came to learn that Nawab was fired at with guns some days ago.)

"What!?" exclaimed Dr.Randhawa in disbelief.

"Sir, it was apparently a case of mistaken identities.Some goons had come to his area to shoot some other guy, but mistook Nawab to be him and shot at him. His injuries are quite serious in nature, but he is recovering now at Dr.Awasthi's hospital.He should be okay and ready to join back here by next week, I suppose," Amrita told.

"See if any help is required by him.Get it done from the Hospital's funds," Dr.Randhawa instructed Amrita and left. "I am going to meet with the trustees today,you carryon," he informed her before leaving.

"Okay,sir," she nodded and left for her work.

At Dr.Awasthi's hospital,room no. 111 had transformed into a site of blossoming romance. Ashika would come to meet Nawab everyday. She took care of all his needs as if he were her beloved. She would bring home-cooked food for him and feed him with her own hands. The hospital nurses were always around to take care of his other needs, but Ashika did not leave his sidefor even a single day.

One day, Ashika was feeding Nawab while no one else was present in the room.She was looking astonishingly beautiful in apink salwar kameez, her hair left loose over her shoulders, and with her remarkable soft and moist lips. She bentforward to feed Nawab with a spoon. Nawab angled his chin up to bring his mouth a little closer towards the spoon.

"*Uff…thoda dard hai* neck *me*," he said. (I feel a little ache in my neck.)

"*Theek hai, khaa lo*," said Ashika (alright, eat something), and bent a little further towards him. While taking the food from the spoon, he lost balance and the empty spoon slipped fromAshika's fingers, and landed with a clang below the bed. In an attempt to catch it, Ashika lunged forward and before she could realize it, her lips came to rest on Nawab's hairy chest. While this happened, Nawab caught sight of the back of Ashika's bare neck and felt butterflies in his stomach. Ashika's breasts rubbed lightly against Nawab's right hand and he felt chills run down his spine. In that span of a few seconds, adrenaline burned both of them with excitement.Unaware of where he got the strength from, he pulled Ashika up and put his lips over hers.

Ashika closed her eyes and did not resist.Both continued to kiss for a few minutes,inseparable for a while. Ashika felt the passion in Nawab's kiss as her eyes blinked open and a smile spread on her face. Nawab looked into her eyes and continued tokiss her.His audacious fingers took the liberty to traverse across Ashika's curves, that sent sensations rushing through her body.

Romance between Nawab and Ashika remained on a high as he eventually recovered in mid April and resumed work at Verma Memorial.Gradually, he took complete charge of thepurchase department. Twice or thrice veryday, an incoming phone call would be transferred from the reception to Nawab's deskand vice versa, an outgoing call would be connected to room no. 011 at Dr.Awasthi's Hospital to Ashika. They talked to each other everyday and met every evening at the decided venue of Shalimar Café.

Monsoon arrived with Nawab's birthday on 5th June. Ashika decided to host him for dinner at her house in Tardeo Worli. As planned, Nawab reached Ashika's house and saw the entire place decorated with the words *Happy Birthday,my Nawab*. She hadn't invited any other people, so it was just the two of them in the room. They had a blast all evening and then sat to have dinner together that lasted till midnight. Nawab finallysaid,"Ashika,*ab nikalta hu…kal milte hain*." (I should leave now…I will see you tomorrow.)

Ashika replied insistingly,"*Ruk jaao naa aaj ki raat yahin.*" (Stay here for the night, won't you?)

Nawab turned to her,looked directly into her eyes and smiled. "*Par mai kahansounga? Sofe par chalega…theek hai, mai sofe par so jaata hun.*"(But where will I sleep? Is it okay if I sleep on the sofa? Alright, I shall sleep on the sofa.)

"*Sofe pe nahi, Nawab.Andar bedroom hai,vahaanso jaao,*" said Ashika. (Not on the sofa. You may sleep inside the bedroom.)

"*Aur aap kaha pe so'oge?*" asked Nawab. (And where will you sleep?)

"*Usi bed pe.Chalo ab der mat karo,*" said Ashika.(On the same bed.Come now, hurry up.)

Nawab didn't know how to react, but he felt happy within. Both moved to the bedroom. Ashika had on a white T-shirt and blue jeans, with her hair falling down to her shoulders,while Nawab was inblack trousers and a white shirt. Ashika took out a pinknightgown from her wardrobe and entered the washroom to change into it. Nawab simply lied down on the bed in the same evening clothes.

A moment later, Ashika came back into the room wearing that pink nightgown. Nawab switched on the radio kept on the table, and the song '*Julie…I love you*' from the recently released movie Julie came on. He started humming along, as Ashika came closer to stand beside him. Nawab could make out from the smooth curving silhouette of her dress that she had nothing on underneath the nightgown. Ashika leaned forward to switch off the lights, while Nawab slowly removed his clothes. Ashika pulled off her gown and drew herself closer to Nawab. He kissed all over her body, his lips travelling fromhead to toe, from back to front, from her toes to knees, lips to neck, and then onto her bosom, to her stomach and thighs, and finally sucked at her destination with his mouth and tongue. He cuddled her between his arms, arousing her andtransporting her to a different world.Nawab stroked her sweet spot and eventually made love to her.

The next morning at 6AM on June 6th, both Nawab and Ashika found themselves in each other's arms in bed."It was the best birthday gift I've ever received, Ashika," said Nawab.

"Hmm…Nawab,*mujhe return gift chahiye*,"demanded Ashika. (I want a return-gift.)

"*Kya chahiye*?" asked Nawab. (What do you want?)

"*Hmm…aaj mera birthday hai,*" she said. (Today is my birthday.)

Nawab kissed her eyes and rekindled the passion from the night before. As it is said, early morning sex is a great exercise and one should always attempt to engage in it before one's routine exercise for a happy day ahead. Nawab and Ashika really burned their calories this time. As opposed to the gentle lovemaking from the previous night, they engaged in high voltage passion in the morning, as if there was no tomorrow.It started in bed, but before either of them could realize it, they were both below the shower,drenched wet, concluding their passionate act.

After exhausting all their energy,they finished their morning routines and had breakfast together before leaving forwork in the same taxi. Nawab dropped her off at Dr.Awasthi's Hospital.

"Eat almonds and jackfruit for a few days. You will regain all the energy you lost today," she said teasingly while getting down from the taxi.

"And you should probably apply a little more concealer on your neck to hide all those love bites," replied Nawab. Ashika melted with a smile and landed a soft kiss on his cheek before leaving. Nawab reached Verma Memorial Hospital in the next few minutes. For the entire day while doing their respective work, both of them only thought of the previous night'sshared passion. Sometimes, it's good to have successive birth dates for a couple in love.

On 25th June, 1975, the then Prime Minister Indira Gandhi imposed an emergency throughout the nation and all freedom guaranteed under the Constitution were curtailed. Her son Sanjay Gandhi was the supremo during the emergency. Political developments during this time had a huge impact on the lives of the people of India, and Nawab and Ashika were no exception.Their meetings and long hand-in-hand walks came under the watchful attention of law enforcers, clouding their minds at all times by the fear of getting detained. In all this, however, their love for each other remained intact.

On 15th August, 1975, Fakhruddin Ali Ahmad, the rubber stamp President of India said in his Independence Day speech, "Emergency is only a passing phase," and cautioned that liberty should never be allowed to 'degenerate into license', but whose liberty was he talking about?The government's or of the nation's people?Nobody knew.

The Bollywood film Sholey had just released, but it received a very dim response initially, since another cult film

Jai Jai Santoshi Maa had come outat the same time. Minerva Theatre had very few guests that night, two among which were Nawab and Ashika. They had chosen to watchSholey and took thebalcony seats A18 and A19. They were happy with the low attendance in the theatre since it gave them a better opportunity to shower love upon each other.Nawab didn't watcheven a single frame of the movie, instead he continuously kissed Ashika while they were inside the cinema hall. Ashika too gave in to Nawab's romantic gestures.

Once the movie was over, they came out of the theatre hall to find some police constables picking up people who had come to watch the film. As fate would have it, Nawab couldn't escape the hustle, but managed somehow to let Ashika get out of the chaos. None of the people had violated any law, nor were they criminals.They simply were regular movie goers, but the police had indeed let 'their liberty degenerate into license'by misusing their power in the name of emergency. All of them were locked up at the Byculla*thaana.* This was the second time that Nawab had met with ill fate for no fault of his own. Ashika waited for Nawab all alone in her apartment, while Nawab spent the night in lock up.

Maintenance of Internal Security Act (MISA) was imposed during the emergency. Though the regime which declared the emergency had self-proclaimed secular credentials, but the reality was a game of thrones with the emergency as a mere tool meant to divide and rule the public, and finish the opposition. Nawab Khan with his Muslim sounding name was falsely booked under MISA and was shown as a member of Jamat-e-Eslam, a banned outfit in those days.He waslodged at the Arthur Road Jail. Theirony was that a man of law was now being tortured by law for no crime committed by him. A flourishing careerwas finished even before it could take off. Through a local lawyer, Ashika somehow arranged for a meeting with Nawab.She cried at her fate.Destiny had brought these two lovers together, and now they were separated by the iron rods of jail.

"*Mere aspataal waalo ko bataa dena mil ke, mai koi gunehgaar nahi hu.Mujhe phasaya gaya hai. Amrita madam ko mil ke sab bata dena.Mai vapas aate hi join ho jaaunga,*" Nawab told Ashika. (Meet with the people at my hospital and tell them that I am not a culprit. I have been framed. Meet Amrita madam and tell her all. I shall join back at the hospital as soon as I return.)

"*Par Nawab, vakil bol raha hai ki jab tak emergency hai, tum bahar nahi aa sakte,*" replied the innocent Ashika. (But Nawab, this lawyer says that you won't be able to come out as long as the emergency lasts.)

"*Allah ki jo marzi. Apna khayaal rakhna,*" replied Nawab. (Whatever may be the Allah's will. You take care of yourself.)

When the meeting time got over, Ashika left the prison and headed straight for Verma Memorial Hospital to meet Amrita.

Ashika sounded every detail of what had been going on to Amrita, who in turn met Dr.Randhawa. Dr.Randhawa wasn't too keen onkeeping Nawab in his employment thereafter and was hesitant to help, but eventually succumbed to Amrita's pressure and convincing that Nawab hadn't broken any rule of law, in fact, he was aman of law and it was theHospital'sresponsibility to support him in thebest way possible. Ashika was impressed and felt obliged at the kind gesture of Amrita and Dr.Randhawa.

Thereafter, each time she went tomeet Nawab in prison, Amrita accompaniedher. On 21st August, 1975, both of them made one such trip to meet Nawab in prison. Amrita had brought along a*rakhi* to tie on Nawab's wrist. On seeing him, she said,"*Nawab bhai, aaj Rakhi hai.Pahale hi din se jab aap aaye the job ke liye hospital me, mujhe laga jese mera bhai aaya hai.*" (Nawab brother,it is Rakhi today.When you had first come to the hospital seeking a job, I felt as if my brother had come.)

Nawab simply looked on while she tied therakhi around his wrist.Ashika stood nearby. "*Tu fikar mat kar. Mai aur Ashika tujhe is narak se nikal lenge, chahe jo ho,*" she assured him. (Don't worry, Ashika and I will do everything to get you out of this hell.)

"*Di…aap apna aur Ashika ka khayal rakhna,*" said Nawab with tears in his eyes. (Sister, you take care of yourself and Ashika.)

"*Aap bhi himmat mat hariye,*" they said and turned to exit the meeting room. (You don't lose hope either.) Ashika turned back towards Nawab and rushed to hold his hand once before leaving, while Amrita waited for her outside the prison. When she came out after a few minutes, they took a taxi to their respective workplaces.

Since then, Amrita and Ashika had developed a special bond with each other. They would both visit Nawab together and shared their life experiences together. On 31st October, 1975, Amrita and Ashika met at Gaylord's, a famous restaurant at Church Gate, at about 6:30 in the evening. As a mark of tribute to the legendary musicianSachin Dev Burman, or'Sachin Da' as he was popularly known, who had died on the same day, a song from the beautiful film Bandini was airing on the Radio,'*Mere Sajan Hai Us Paar,Mai Is Par.Oh Mere Majhi Ab Ki Baar Le chal Paar.*'Bandini' was a magical masterpiece in black and white by the legendary director Bimal Roy. It was the story of a love-triangle between three characters played by Dada Muni(Ashok Kumar), Dharmendra and Nutan.

Ashika and Amrita were having a quiet dinner while listening to the song. Curiously, Ashika asked Amrita,"*Aap kisi ko pyar nahi karte? Kuch batao naa aap ke bare me.Maine to aap ko ab tak sab bata hi diya hai pichle do mahine me, par aap khud ke baare me kuch nahi batatin.*" (Don't you love someone? Tell me something about yourself. I have told you all about me in the last two months, but you don't tell me anything about yourself.)

Amrita smiled and replied, "*Aaaa…dil. Aadil hai naam uska.*" (His name is Aadil.)

"*Kaise mile, kahan mile?*"asked Ashika more curiously. (Where and how did you meet him?)

"Hmm," Amrita took a long pause, then started…

It was June 1st, 1970.The city of Mumbai sees thousands of peoplewith dreams in their eyes pouring into it everyday from across the country. Out of those thousand people who landed at V.T. Station that day, one was a girl who stepped out ofCalcutta Mail. She dreamt of becoming a doctor, a gynaecologist, but destiny had written something else for her.It was Amrita…AmritaBanerjee - a girl from a modest middle-class family from West Bengal.

While the passengers of Calcutta Mail were slowly alighting frombogie no. S11,a beautiful girl with hair reaching down to her shoulders got down with a little luggage and straightened her yellow sari while looking around, a little scared and confused. She came out of the V.T.Station near the taxi lane, where a speeding cab haltednext to her. Amrita looked at the taxi-walah (driver) astonished.

Peeping out of the taxi window, the driver asked, "Kaha chalna hai, memsa'b? (Madam, where do you want to go?)

Amrita took out a chit from her purse and read,"Women's Hostel,Peddar Road."

"Aao, baith jao."(Come on, sit.)

"Ka…ka kitne paise honge?" Amrita asked nervously. (How much will the fare be?)

"Yahi koi…do rupaye.Chalna hai?" (Just about two Rupees.Coming?)

Amrita said yes and got into the taxi.

The taxi-walah looked at her in the rear view mirror and asked,"Pehli baar aaee hain kya Bombai me?" (Have you come to Mumbai for the first time?)

"Oh, yes," Amrita replied while looking at the sea near Marine Lines. "Doctor ki padhai karne, yahi Verma Memorial Hospital me." (To study medicine here at Verma Memorial Hospital.)

"Doctor ki padhai, bahut paisa kharach hua hoga," commented the driver. (It must be very expensive studying medicine here.)

"Han, lagta hai,"she replied nonchalantly. (Yes, I guess so.)

"Bombai me sambhal ke rahana. Ye lo, aapka hostel aagaya." (Be careful in Mumbai. Here, we have reached your hostel.)

Amritalooked out of the window to see the hostel board, then said after taking a pause, "Kitne paise hue?" (How much is the fare?)

"Do rupaye," replied the taxi-walah. (Two Rupees.)

Amrita tookthe money out from her purse to give to the taxi-walah and got down.

The next day,a handsome young man was having coffeeat Madras Café near Parel Railway Station.The restaurant manager was busy with his work at the counter while enjoying songs on the radio. This man finished his coffee and went to the manager to ask,"Ek coffee, kitne paise?" (One Coffee, how much?)

The manager answered, "Chaar aana. Aap kya student lagta hai idhar kahin ka?" (Four aanas. Are you a student here somewhere?)

"Yahin, Verma Memorial Hospital me medical student," replied the young man named Aadil Hussain.

"Idharich baaju me - first left, aur phir second right," informed the manager. (It's right here, first left and then the second right.)

Aadil took out some money from his pocket and gave it to the manager before leaving. There was a bus stop right outside the restaurant, where a bus came to a stop and Amrita alighted from it. She asked one of the bystanders, an old man, where this Verma Memorial Hospital was."Take the first left, and then the second right," replied the old man.

Aadil, who had been standing right next to the old man, looked at Amrita. She movedin the direction of the hospital and Aadil followed her. She realized soon that someone was following her,so she slowed down for a while and letAadil take over and move ahead.When he crossed her,Amrita looked at him angrily and said,"Idiot."

Aadil heard it, but ignored the comment.He reached the hospital in ten minutes, followed by Amrita behind him. All new students assembled in the lecture room at the hospital. Dr. Jagmohan Randhawa and the Chairman of trustees enter the room and the students get up to greet them.

Dr. Randhawa asks the students to sit down and introduces Dr. Wadia, theChairman, to the students.

The Chairmanwelcomes the students and announces, "Keeping with the tradition of m/s Verma Memorial Hospital,we have shortlisted five students amongst you all toreceive the scholarship from m/s Verma Memorial Trust. This selection was done on the basis of academic achievements as well as the economic condition of the students who applied." He then asked Dr. Randhawa to announce the list.

Dr. Jagmohan Randhawa took the mike and looked at all the students. He started,"After the announcement,all the shortlisted students are requested to meet with Dr. Wadia at 2.00 p.m. for administrative requirements."He then announced each name on the list, which included Aadil and Amrita's name too.

Soon after the assembly was dismissed, Aadilasked all the scholarship holders, "Can we all please have coffee together?"

Everyone agreed in unison, "Yeah, why not?" Amrita remained silent. Everyone except Amritaheaded for the hospital canteen.

Aadillooked at Amrita and said,"Why are you not coming?Please join us."

Amrita simply looked at Aadil and headed to the canteen with him. At the canteen, all the five students took a table where Aadil and Amrita took seats facing each other. Aadil called for a waiter and ordered some snacks and coffee.He introduced himself first to all the fellow students,"Hi, I am Aadil."

The only other boy shook hands with him and said, "Hi, I am Rahul."

They looked at the three girls then and prompted, "Hey girls, please introduce yourselves."

The waiter arrived just then with the snacks and coffee.

The first two girls, Nafisa and Pritha, introduced themselves, Amrita going at the last,"I am Amrita from Calcutta."

All of them got well acquainted with each other over the snacks and coffee.

At the hostel that night, Amrita was lying in bed with a pen and a piece of paper in her hand. She was writing a letter to her mother, informing her about her selection for the Verma Memorial Trust scholarship. She wrote:

"Dear mom, I have reached here safely. Today was the first day of my college and you will be pleased to know that I have been selected for the scholarship. I have made some new friends here, like Nafisa, Pritha, Rahul and Aadil. You needn't worry about me. I will keep writing to you.Now that you have become the Principal, your workload must have increased too. Just take it easy, and don't rush. Once I become a doctor, I shall take care of everything."

Calcutta (now Kolkata) has forever been and still is the city of joy. Somewhere in the salt lake area, there was a tiny badi (house) where Amrita's mother lived. When she received and read Amrita's letter, she started laughing. A servant working nearby asked curiously, "Tumi hasacha kena?"(Why are you laughing?)

Amrita's mother replied, still laughing, "Aami parachi Amrita chitthi." (I am reading Amrita's letter.)

"Kya likhaa hai?" asked the servant.(What has she written?)

"Likha hai, jab vo doctor banjayegi, sab kuch sambhal legi." (She has written that once she becomes a doctor, she will take care of everything.)

"Theek hi to kaha hai.Isme hasne ki kya baat hai?" asked the servant. (What she says is correct.What's there to laugh?)

The mother chided, "Aree budhu, uski padhai ke baad mai uski shaadi karwa dungi.Hamare yahan beti jab sasuraal jaati hai, to uske ghar paani bhi pina thik nahi samjhte.Rivaz nahi hai." (You idiot, once she finishes her studies, I will get her married.In our culture, when daughters go to their in-laws, we can't even accept water there.)

"Oye dayya, aami to bhuli gayo," replied the servant bashfully. (Oh, god. I completely forgot.)

***

Ashika and Amrita had almost finished their dinner at the Gaylord's in Church Gate. Amrita finally said, "After finishing our course atVerma Memorial Hospital, some students left to pursue further studies abroad. Rahul left too, as he got invited by another institute for an internship. However,Aadil, Nafisa,Pritha and Igot offered an internship right here at the Verma Memorial Hospital, which will hopefully get over by next year."

She continued after a pause, "It has been almost five years since we got here. All of us have developed a special bonding between us.Every summer, we went to our respective houses for vacation, but when we're here we do group studies, play games, debate, go for picnics, pass time over conversations and exchangenotes together like any other group of students in a college.While studying together,Aadil and I had initially developed a liking for each other, which later blossomed into a romance." Amrita took a long pause now.

"Hmm…" said Ashika smilingly.They paid the bill and left the restaurant. "You can stay over at my place tonight," offered Ashika.

"Alright, let's go," replied Amrita and they both headed forWorli, where Ashika's apartment was.

In the afternoon of 1stNovember, 1975,the day of Dhanteras, Ashika and Amrita managed to get Nawab released from prison with the help of an advocate, and immediately reached Byculla prison to complete the release formalities. It was a Saturday and they were engrossed in the completion of his release ordersby the court all day. By six in the evening, Nawab was out of prison and saw thesunset as a free man once again. He felt extremely relieved,as did Ashika and Amrita.

They all took a taxi and headed to Ashika's house in Worli.She had prepared dinner for everyone at home. At about nine at night, after they had finished dinner, Amrita said, "I should leave for hostel now."

"Di, it's quite late in the night now. Why don't you stay here?" Nawab insisted, while Ashika looked at Amrita and joined in, "Yes, please stay here."

Amrita smiled and wenttoanother room with Ashika at her tail. "I got my periods today and I have mentioned this to Nawab. Nothing of what you are thinking is going to happen tonight anyway. You should stay," Ashika revealed to Amrita.

Amrita smiled and they both burst out laughing. Amrita stayed back at Ashika's house that night and returnedthe next day on 2nd November, 1975,the day justbefore Diwali. Before she left, they all wished each other Diwali and exchanged their best wishes.3rd November, 1975, was the first Diwali that Ashika and Nawab got to spend with each other.

On the morning of 4th November, Amrita was in her hostel room when a postman entered the hostel hurriedly. The security watchman asked him, "*Kidhar jana hai?*" (Where do you want to go?)

The postman replied,"*Amrita Banerjee ka telegram hai.*" (There is a telegram for Amrita Banerjee.)

"*Thik hai, ek mint,*" said the watchman. (Alright, one minute.) He then called a ground staff and instructed, "*Inko Amrita madam ka room dikhao.*" (Show him to Amrita madam's room.)

Amrita was getting ready for work when suddenly her doorbell rang.She rushed to open the door to find the staff member outside. He said,"*Madam, aapke liye telegram hai.*" (Madam, there is atelegram for you.)

Amrita was shocked.She received the telegram from the postman and hurriedly signed the paper before starting to read it. The contents of the telegram shocked and upset her. She immediately went down to where the hostel phone was and dialledDr. Randhawa. When she could not connect to him, she called Dr.Wadia directly.

Dr. Wadiapicked up the phone and greeted,"Hello,Dr. Wadia speaking."

Amrita stuttered, “Dr…aa…Amrita.”

“What happened, Amrita? Why are you so scared?”

Amrita composed herself and spoke in a rushed manner, “Doctor, my mother is in a serious condition. It’s urgent. I will have to go to Calcutta right now. I was trying to call Dr.Randhawa, but I guess there is some problem, I could not connect to him.”

"Okay, okay, relax, don’t worry. I will inform him.If you need any help with the money or anything…”

“Thanks doctor, I have the money,” she said and putdown the telephone receiver.

The next morning, Calcutta Mail dashed into Howrah Junction, carrying Amrita in it. She rushed to her salt lake abode, only to find that her mother had passed away. She took care of the funeral proceedings with the help of her relatives and spent the next few days at her family’s salt lake hose. In the hurried move from Bombay to Calcutta, she had been unable to inform Aadil of the news. There was no way to inform him now since neither had a personal phone line and as interns, they could only use the phone at the hospital to connect. This phone too was only available during the working hours, beyond which there was no means for them to stay in touch.

Two weeks passed by since Aadil hadlast seen Amrita. This was the first time that Aadil had been away from Amrita for a period of more than a week. For the first time in their five years long courtship,Aadil felt that he was not able to concentrate on his work. He had no clue of Amrita’s whereabouts and started to worry. He finally enquired with Nafisa and Pritha about her, “Where is Amrita? Do you have any idea?”

"No yaar, we don’t know,” said Nafisa.

"She didn't say anything to anyone before disappearing.Perhaps Dr.Randhawa or Dr.Wadia would know where she is,"suggested Pritha.

"How?" asked Aadil.

"If she has taken a leave for this long, she would have submitted a leave application to them,"reasoned Nafisa.

"Alright, bye. I'll catch up with you later," said Aadil and left.

Nafisa turned to Pritha and asked,"Why is he so worried about Amrita?"

"You should know why a boy gets worried about a girl," replied Pritha mischievously.

Aadil reached outside Dr. Wadia's cabin, but felt hesitant to go in. 'How should I ask him about Amrita? What if he suspects that something is going on between us?' he wondered, then changed his mood.'Leave it.It's not right. But how do I find out where she is? No.'Tormented by his thoughts, he made his way to his department.

Aadil realises that he was missing Amrita quite intensely. He was confused and worried. He wondered whether he was only missing her presence, or if it was something else between them. He had no answer to this. 'Maybe no, could be yes.' He knew that he was in love with her, and so was she with him, yet there were so many unanswered questions in between. He spent many sleep-less nights during that time, just thinking about Amrita.

After two weeks, Amrita returned to the hospital. Every morning during that time,Aadil had waited hopelessly for her at the café next to the bus-stop.Finally, at 10 a.m. that day,the bus arrived andAadil saw a familiar face getting down with utmost grace and elegance. It was his Amrita and he shouted as soon as he recognised her,"Amrita…Amrita…Amrita."

Amrita turnedaroundto look at Aadil, but remained silent. Aadil ran up to her and said, "Where have you been?You didn't even bother to inform me before leaving. Do you even know what I havebeen through? But why am I telling all this to you, aah…"

Amrita still remained silent and seemed unwilling to respond.

Irritated by her silence, Aadil finally said, "Alright, if you don't want to tell me, that's okay. Who am I to you anyway? Nobody.And what the hell are you to me?Nothing."He took a brief pause, then resumed, "Sorry, I am really sorry.You mean a lot to me…I am sorry!"

Amritainterrupted him, "I had gone to my mother's funeral,"while looking straight into his eyes.

Aadil was stunned.He realized his mistake and was unable to meet her gaze. Instead, he simply looked down apologetically. Amrita turned around and started walking towards the hospital.Aadil simply looked on while she walked away.

Nawab greeted Amrita at the hospital when he saw her. "Di, long time no see. Is every thing alright?"he asked while sipping onhis tea in her cabin.

"Bhai,my mother is no more," she replied morosely.

"*Allah unhe jannat bakshe*," said Nawab. (May God grant her heaven.) "I will see you later, you take care of yourself," he said as he got up to leave. He had just reached the cabin's door when a ward boy came running in and said, "*Sa'ab, aapke table pe koi Ashika madam ka phone hai.*"(Sir, some Ashika madam has called you at your table.) Amrita looked at Nawab and smiled.

"You should marry her. She is a good girl. I will be very pleased," Amrita said to Nawab.

"*Insha Allah,* I shall marry her, di," replied Nawab and turnedaround to touch her feet and take her blessings.

"Come on, what is this?" said Amrita, and an emotional Nawab left her cabin without another word.

“Hello?” said Nawab, pickingup the telephone receiver at his desk. “Hello? Say something. Ashika Nawab Kha…”

“What? What did you say?”asked Ashika astonished.

“Ashika Nawab Khan,” repeated Nawab.“Do you mind taking on this name?”
“No,” she said.

“Di says I should marry you,” continued Nawab. “I will come meet you tonight. We’ll sit together and discuss the rest. I have a lot of work pending here right now.”

“Alright, let’s meet tonight. Allah hafiz,” said Ashika.

Pritha,Nafisa and Amrita werehaving snacks and tea at the hospital canteen, but Amrita was unusually quiet.

While taking a sip of her tea, Nafisa said, “Relax Amrita, we are all here with you. I know that we can’t replace your mother, but don’t ever feel that your are alone in this world.”

Amrita just game them a silent yet pained smile in return.

"Take it easy, Amrita,” comforted Pritha.

Aadil was waiting outside the canteen. He had no guts to go in and face Amrita after than morning. He knew that Amrita was sitting inside with Pritha and Nafisa.He had seen them having tea together from outside the canteen. After they were done, Amrita, Pritha and Nafisa got up and started walking towards the canteen's entrance door. Still feeling quite hesitant, Aadil turned around and started walking slowly. When the girls exited the canteen, he pretended to not having seen them.

When Nafisa spotted him, she called out his name. Aadil turned around to face them.

"We haven't seen you since this morning," said Nafisa.

Aadillooked at Amrita and said, "Yeah, it's nothing." Amrita pretended to ignore him and looked away.

Pritha pointed to the two of them and exclaimed, "Hey, why are you two not talking to each other? Have you both had a quarrel?"

"Nooo," interjected Aadil, "but…"

Amrita and Aadil exchanged a look. Aadil soon resumed, "Amrita, I am really sorry. I didn't know.Please forgive me."

Pritha and Nafisa looked on hesitantly as he fell to Amrita's knees.

"Hey, what is all this? Please get up! I have no issues with you," exclaimed Amrita.

Aadil got up hurriedly and said thank you. "Let's have tea," he continued while pointing towards the canteen.

"We have already had tea," Nafisa and Pritha said teasingly. "If you two want to go have some again, please do."

"No, I don't want to," said Amrita.

Aadil shook his head confusedly and proceeded towards the canteen dejected. Amrita, Pritha and Nafisa started walkingin the opposite direction.

"Aaha, someone is blushing," teased Nafisa.

"What…?" Amrita said, surprised.

Pritha andNafisa started singing the popular song'*Pyar hua, ikarar hua, fir pyar se kyun darta hai dil*' from the movie Shree 420.

Just then, they saw Nawab walking towards the canteen.

"*Arre yaar*, the moment I see this tall and handsome guy,my heart starts beating like crazy.But he is so arrogant, he only talks to Amrita," said Nafisa while looking at Pritha.

"Ohh, shut up," said Amrita, "*Bhai* has a girlfriend."

"*Aadab*, Khan sa'ab," said Nafisa as they drew closer to him.

"*Aadab,*" said Nawab politely and continued while looking at Amrita, "How are you, *di*?"

"I am alright.How is Ashika?" she asked in return.

"She is fine," said Nawab and smiled.

"Ashika…hmm," teased Nafisa."The arrogant man has cracked a smile for the first time."

This made everyone laugh.

Back at the hostel room,Amrita was lying in her bed. The ceiling fan of her room was on and she was thinking something. She had millions of questions going on in her mind, and all these questions were related to Aadil. She was asking herself,*Is this the right time to ask Aadil about marriage?* In the last five years, they had moved on from a mere friendship to a full-fledged relationship. 'Why did Aadil say that I meant a lot to him? Is he ready for marriage? Why did he behave like that this morning, as if he belongs to me? Or may be, he has the right to behave like that.' Amrita regrettednot informing Aadil of her mother's deteriorating health before leaving to Calcutta! 'How could I have told him anything?Everything happened so quickly and in such haste,' she asked herself. 'Is Aadil very angry with me over this?' So many questions poured into Amrita's mind, but she could not find an answer.

She wondered whether he genuinely loved her. Even if he did, there were so many reservations based on their difference in religion that made her hesitate in thinking about marriage. She knew that their community would never allow them to marry. It was just not possible in the conservative and hypocrite society that they lived in. Perhaps all this would have been irrelevant had she been more powerful, she thought, and more than just economically. It did not matter to her on a personal level as an individual, but it did to certain people of the so called'society'.

At 2:30 A.M., Amrita was still awake and staring at the ceiling fan that was mirroring in its rotation the questions in her mind.

The same night, Nawab and Ashika had gone out for some ice cream at Hazi Ali after having finished dinnerat Ashika's house. They sat near the sea-facing Hazi Ali dargaah in Worli. Theemergency hadn't been lifted yet, and at about 10:30 PM, a constable approached them and askedthem to go home, so they did. Though it was the last week of November, Bombay wasn't as cold as it generally got in winters. Both of them had a shower and went to bed together.Lights were put out as they took their sides on the bed.Nawab was still awake, but Ashika was quickly losing consciousness. Nawab turned to Ashika and put a hand on her breast.He started cuddling it, pressing her nipples while at it.

"Ouchh!Idiot," she reacted and turned to put her head over Nawab's chest. He was excited to burn some calories, but restrained himself as he understood that Ashika was fast sleep in his arms.

India was in a state of political turmoil at the same time due to the imposition of emergency. Jai Prakash Narayan who hadbeen detained in Chandigarh, was released on unconditional parole in mid-November, 1975, due to deteriorating health conditions, and was admitted to Jaslok Hospital in Bombay.On diagnosis, it was revealed that JP (as he was affectionatelycalled) hadkidney failure and required dialysis for the rest of his life. A man of the masses, a stalwart leader who had united the entire country under his movement of *Sampoorn Kranti-* total revolution, was lying lifeless in a bed at Jaslok Hospital. Many prominent leaders from across the country came to visit the ailing JP, including Indira Gandhi who received a cold shoulder from everyone on her visit to Jaslok Hospital.

The year was to end in a few weeks to begin a new era. Christmas and New Year's Eve came and went quietly, since the environment was not conducive for happening parties, but the motley group of employees from Verma Memorial Hospital decided to celebrate New Year's Eve and the host was Nawab Khan this time.

Noorani Manzil witnessed a few guests entering into Nawab's house - a tiny apartment in the stinking by-lanes of Nagpada. Everyone from Amritato Adil, to Nafisa, Pritha,Anna, and Ashika were present at his house. This was the first time that Aadil was interacting with Nawab closely since he had learned that Amrita treated him like a brother and that he was always present at her behest. At about 10 PM when all of them were having dinner together, Ashika started feeling a little uneasy and excused herself to go to the washroom.No sooner had she entered, she started vomiting.She came back and informed Amrita about it, while Nawab looked on. Amrita in turn whispered the same into Nafisa's ears,while Aadil who had been sitting next to Amrita, understood what was going on.

He got up from his chair and hugged Nawab.

"Nawab Khan sa'ab,take care of Ashika.She is pregnant," Nafisa said teasingly.

Amrita smiled too and said, "Brother, you two should get married now."

"Yes,*di*. But there is one more thing."

Both Ashika and Amrita looked at him in surprise. He held Aadil's hand and brought it together withAmrita's. "You two should also consider it for yourselves," he said and continued, "We all know and see it."

Everyone started clapping. Aadil and Amrita found themselves speechless and stunned. All of them partied till midnight, greeted each other, then left the next morning.

1976 begin on a glorious note as Nawab and Ashika decided to formalize their relationship and the first week of January went smoothly. On 8th January, 1976, the then President of India suspendedtheseven (now only six) freedoms guaranteed under Article 19 of the Constitution of India.In another couple of weeks, i.e. on 24th January 1976, Parliament of India approved the ordinance that took away the powers of court to ask for reasons behind detention under MISA(Maintenance of Internal Security Act).

On the same morning, 24th January, 1976, Dagdu Aandhale was to join Verma Memorial Hospital as a ward boy. Of the thousands of hutments established in Dharavi - India's largest slum, one belonged to him. After pumping air in the tyres of his bicycle and making sure that they were fit to ride on, he deposited the air pump back in his hutment, took out aShivaji *bidi* from his shirt pocket on the left, lit it and paddled off. His bicycle came out onto the road that led to the hospital.

The Chairman of Verma MemorialHospital ringed Dr. Jagmohan Randhawa, the dean, early that morning.

"Good morning, sir," greeted Dr. Randhawa.

"Good morning,doctor. I am sending a boy named Dagdu Aandhale today. He has been recommended by our trustee *bhausaheb.*Please accommodate him in some department," said the Chairman.

"What are his qualifications, sir?"

"I think he is matric pass."

"Okay, sir.We do need a ward boy in the GynaecologyDepartment. I will take care of it."

"Thank you and bye," said the Chairman and hung up.

Dagdu Aandhale entered the hospital and headed straight for Dr. Jagmohan Randhawa's cabin. Dr. Randhawa picked up the intercom and asked the receptionist to send Amrita in. He then turned to Dagdu and asked, "When did you pass matric?"

"*Che baras hua,*" said Dagdu. (It has been six years.)

"*Kahan se ho…Bombay kab aye?*"asked Dr. Randhawa again. (Where are you from? When did you come to Bombay?)

"*Ahamad Nagar.Ek hapta hua Bombay aaye.*" (Ahamad Nagar. I arrived in Bombay only a week ago.)

Just then, somebody knocked on Dr. Randhawa's cabin door.

"Come in," he instructed.

"Good morning, doctor," said Amrita, entering his office.

"Good morning,Amrita. This is Dagdu Aandhale. He is to work under you in your department from today. Please take him."

Dagdu looked at Amrita hesitantly as she said, "Okay, sir."

Dr. Randhawa instructed Dagdu, "*Jao,doctor memsa'ab kaam samjhadengi, aur suno, mujhe koi shikayat nahi aani chahiye tumhare baare me.*" (Go,doctor madam will explain your work to you, and listen, I don't want any complaints about you.)

"Yes,sir," said Dagdu andleft the room with Amrita.

Later that day, Amrita waschecking some report in her department of Gynaecology. Upon completion, she rushed towards the patient's ward and asked Dagdu Aandhale to follow her. He was to assist her in the routine check-ups of her patients.

Dr. Aadil was just emerging out of the operation theatre then and was running down to the Neurosurgery Department with Dr. Wadia. Both of them were in conversation over a medical report.

Handing over the report to Aadil, Dr. Wadia said, "Doctor, pleasestudy through this report thoroughly, I want feedback immediately."

"Okay, doctor," Aadil responded.

Dr. Amrita along with Dagdu Aandhale met these two at the staircase.

"Hello,doctor.How are you?" Dr. Wadia greeted Amrita, then turned to look at Dagdu in confusion.

"This is Dagdu Aandhale," Amrita started. "He has joined my department from today." She then turned to Aadil and said, "Hi, doctor. How about you?"

"Alright," said Aadil.

They crossed each other on the stairs.While passing Amrita, Aadil suddenly turned and they both smiled at each other.

"Hello,*di.*" Nawab stood at the top of the stairs and found Amrita blushing as she made her way past Aadil.

"How are you,brother?" she asked him.

"I am good. I have decided to marry Ashika next week on the day of *jummah*," he told her.

"Oh…on 31st January? That's so nice," she reacted excitedly and hugged him. Dagdu remained standing beside her while she spoke to Nawab, who didn't ask her anything about him. "You all have to come attend it. I will give you the details later. The ceremony is right here inMazgaon.I will meet up with you in the evening. I have a lot of work pending right now," said Nawab and moved on to see to his work.

"Let's go," Amrita instructed Dagdu and headed for the ward.

Back in her cabin later, she was glancing through some files in her rack, while Dagdu was standing behind her, continuously staring at the back of her neck. His lusty eyes were screening her entire frame and buttocks. Unaware of this, she turned around and instructed him, "Give me that file," while pointing at a file on her desk. He remained staring at her assets, keeping his gaze fixed on the skin that he could see above the rim of her blouse. "Can you not hear me?" she raised her voice and drew Dagduout of his dream hesitantly.

"Yes, madam. Here," he said as he picked up the file from her table. Taking the file, she deposited herself in a chair and started reading through it, unaware still about the lust in Dagdu's eyes. "Go to the Store Department and get me the stock list from there," she instructed Dagdu again.

"Yes, madam," he said and lefther cabin.

In the morning of the Republic day, 1976, Nafisa had just finished her morning tea and was glancing through the newspaper. Her gaze fell upon the photograph of a handsome man whom she recognised as Dr. Shezad Afridi, originally from the mango town of Malihabad -the majestic tehsil of Lucknow. Malihabad was just an hour's drive from Lucknow and was the land of legends such as the famous poet Josh Malihabadi, Padmashree Ghaus Mohammad Khan (the first Indian to reach Wimbledon quarter finals), the philosopher Wali Kamal Khan Afreedi, the great horticulturist Abdul Bari Khan Afridi, and Pandit Saiyad Hussain Shastri -the great Sanskrit scholar. Besides these legends, Malihabad was known for its Dussehri breed of mangoes.

It was largely the presence of Afridi pathans in the area that lend identity to the town and gave it a sense of mystery as well. It was believed that the Afridi pathans' settlement in Malihabad dated back to AD 1202.

Dr.Shezad Afridi and Nafisa had been childhood buddies from Malihabad.Their teenage infatuation for each other had blossomed into aromancewhile they studied together at Lucknow Christian College, but they had hadto part when Dr.Shezad left for California in 1970 to pursue further studies in medicine, and Nafisa came to Mumbai.

Dr.Shezad hailed from the renowned family of Shahabad and Sabina Afridi in Malihabad, who had established themselves in mango farming.Being the only child in his family then,all his wishes prevailed over his doting parents. Somehow, his parents did not like Nafisa's presence in his life,and the best way to keep them apart was for them to send him abroad for studies. Nafisa knew the reason behind it, but didn't protest for the sake of her love towards Dr.Shezad.Moreover, she knew verywell that her protests would not bring back her love.

That day, she could not take her eyes off the picture in the newspaper where Dr.Shezad stood in the company of a gorgeous lady mentioned as Mrs. Shezad Afridi, while receiving an award at a function held at the Delhi Golf Club. Her eyes welled up and a drop fell from them onto the picture of her ex-beloved. She got up, threw the newspaper in the dustbin and headed towards the bath to takea shower. She undressed herself, stood beneath the flowing water and closed her eyes.

***

In Fayaz Ganj,Chandni Chowk, Delhi,the household ofShaikh family was engaged in the last-minute preparations before leaving for Mumbai for their daughter's second wedding. Traditionally, pre-wedding rituals such as *Manjha* and *Mehandi* ceremony ought to have taken place at this house, but it was a hush–hush marriage between Nawab and Ashika, so these ceremonies were going to be conducted at Ashika's house in Bombay for everyone's convenience. With only two days remaining before the

*Nikaah*ceremony, the Shaikh family had to reach there somehow by 27th January. All of them boardedthe Punjab Mail boundfor Mumbai.

The next morning, Ashika and Nawab came to receive them at Mumbai Central. Ashika introduced Nawab to her father, mother and younger brother. From there, they headed straightto Ashika's housein Worli. Rituals from thebride's side commenced the same evening. Amrita remained with the family all along, taking lead in arranging all the last minute requirements for the rituals with the help of Ashika's mother.

At Noorani Manzil, Nawab was all alone.He was expecting Aadil to come stay with him that night and help him arrangeeverything before the *Nikaah* ceremony. Aadil reached his place late at night, at about 11 PM, and they both sat down to have dinner first which Nawab had already prepared for them. Nawab and Aadil were spending time in each other's company exclusively for the first time, so it was only natural that they talked more about their past rather than the upcoming wedding.

"You should get married to*di* soon," Nawab told Aadil.

"Hmm, I have thought about it," replied Aadil. "Once your wedding is over, I will travel to Bhopal to discuss it."

"Who stays in Bhopal?" Nawab asked curiously.

"*Ammi*and *Abbu*," replied Aadil, and they both went on talking past midnight.

Aadil knew everything about Nawab, since Amrita had told him all about him.Thus, it was now his turn to tell Nawab about his life in Bhopal.

HabibGanj, Bhopal, had a largemansion spread over five acres of land and was known as Abdullah Mansion, named after Mr.Abdullah Hussain - a wealthy businessman who ran a transport company and owned more than a hundred trucks. For a family, Mr.Abdullah had a wife named Sakina Bi, Aadil - the elder son, and Sadik - the younger son.

Aadil had always been good in studies, so he pursued his education, while Sadik preferred to support his father in his transport business. The Hussain family was very traditional and conservative, hence Aadil had not informed them of Amrita yet. His initial schooling had happened at Scindia School, Gwalior, just 425 kilometers away from Habib Ganj.

He had always been a man of few words, and had preferred to remain aloof and devoid of too many friends all through his school days. Upon the completion of his schooling, he came to Mumbai for further studies at Ramnarain Ruia College, Matunga, and joined Verma Memorial Hospital for his studies in medicine thereafter.His parents always supported him in his educational pursuits,while Aadil being an obedient child, only went by his parents'wishes. All along his journey from Habib Ganj to Scindia School, Gwalior, to Ruia college in Mumbai, he had never fallen for any girl. But that was all before he had met Amrita. It wasn't easy for him to convince his conservative parents to let him marry a Hindu brahmin girl from Calcutta.

While Aadil was expressing his life story to Nawab, the latter dozed off.

"Hey buddy, you've fallen asleep while I am going on blabbering here," yelled Aadil.

"No, no. I am listening," Nawab replied in a sleepy tone.

"It's 3 AM already. No wonder. I should sleep now too," said Aadil and went to sleep.

On 31st January, the day of thewedding, the venue near Mazgaon dock looked mesmerising.All the guest had arrived soon after the bride's family. From Nawab's side,the entire staff of Verma Memorial Hospital had been invited. Everyone showed up to grace the event; all except Nafisa. Aadil remained with Nawab all along, helping him with the wedding preparations. The *maulvi* reached the venue at about 5:30 PM and the*Nikaah* ceremony started.After some initial rituals, the*maulvi* sought the bride and the groom's consent to accept each other as husband and wife. The three sacred words'*qubool hai, qubool hai qubool hai*' were exchanged between them and they became husband and wife. Since the emergency hadn't been lifted and the wedding had also been planned in such a hurry, it was decided to hold*walima* the same day. Consequently, the *nikaah* ceremony was followed by *walima* the same evening after 8:00 PM, and was concluded post midnight. Nawab and Ashika sought the blessings of their lovedones and relatives.

The next day, all the guests departed from Ashika's house in Worli. Aadil and Amrita saw Nafisa at the hospital. "Why didn't you come to Nawab's wedding?" asked Aadil while Amrita stood by.

"I had some urgent work to attend to, so I couldn't make it there," she replied. "Alright then, I'll see you later," she said hurriedly and moved away.

"What happened to her?" Aadil asked Amrita.

"Don't know," she replied.

Alright, let's both get to our work," Aadil said and moved on to attend to his assignments, while Amrita smiled and preceded to her cabin.

On the eve of 3rd February, 1976, Nawab and Ashika made their way to Victoria Terminus to catch the Punjab Mail that was scheduled to leave at 6:40 PM.They were waiting for Amrita and Aadil to reach before they could board the train. Just fifteen minutes before departure, both of them reached and greeted the newly married couple, wishing them the best for their honeymoon.

"Nainital is a wonderful place.I am sure you two will enjoy your honeymoon," said Amrita to Nawab and Ashika. Aadil gave Nawab a hug, patted his back and said, "Take care." The couple boarded the train, while Amrita and Aadil left the station.

Nawab and Ashika reached Nainital, the renowned hill station of Uttar Pradesh (now in Uttarakhand), the next dayaccording to their pre-decided honeymoon plans.Hotel Evelyn on Mall Road received two guests from Bombay who stayed there for a whole week. During that week of honeymooningin Nainital, Nawab and Ashika indulged in such love and lust as if there was no tomorrow.

Back in Dharavi,Dagdu Aandhale was having a conversation with an acquaintance named Alok Rai at a pan shop.

"*Maal milega bajane ko*?" asked Dagdu. (Can I get a girl to screw?)

"*Milega,budget bata kitna hai?*" asked Alok. (Sure, what's your budget?)

"Hmm,Rs. 5 to Rs. 10."

"Alright."

"*Maal mast chaahiye.*" (I need the best girl.)

"*Bhinchod, 5 rupaye me heroine chahiye tujhe?Bhaag saale!*" exclaimed Alok. (Sister fucker,you want an Actress for 5 rupees? Get lost!)

"*Thik hai, thik hai, kab milega?*" asked Dagdu. (Alright,alright, when can I have her?)

"*Aaj raat aaja Bhiwandi saath me, mera night duty hai.Bandobast karat hun.*" (Come to Bhiwandi along with me tonight. I will arrange something for you. I have a night duty today.)

Dagdu asked the pan shop owner what the time was, and he replied, "7:15."

"*Tu aadhe ghante me nake pe mil, saath chalte hai,*" assured Alok. (Meet me at the circle in half an hour, we will leave together.)

"*Ho,*" said Dagdu and left.

After about half an hour,Dagdu met Alok at the decided spot and they headed for Bhiwandi together. Alok was originally from Phoolpur in Allahabad, Uttar Pradesh. He came from an army background with most of his family members serving in the force, but he had left the army after only a few years of serviceto come to Bombay. His wife and a little kid still lived back in Phoolpur. In Bombay, he had joined as a security guard at Bhiwandi hosiery unit, and indulged in pimp work for a local sex worker on the side.

At about 11PM, both of them reached the Bhiwandi bus stop from whereAlok led Dagduto a red light area just a little distance away. There, he introduced him to a brothel owner, a raunchy woman.

"*Kya be, ye fantus kaun hai?*" asked the owner. (Who is this joker?)

"*Dost hai, isko maal chaiye,*" explained Alok. (He is a friend, hewants a girl.)

"*Ekdum kawala maal,*" beamed Dagdu. (I want a virgin.)

"*Chutiye…kaunsi randi kawali hoti hai?*" exclaimed the woman and started laughing. (Rascal, which prostitute is a virgin?)

Alok smiled at Dagdu and said, "*Arre, maza karne aaya hai, kar le.*" (You've come to have fun,just go ahead.)

"Money?" asked the brothel owner. Dagdu handed her 15 rupees from his pocket.

"My share?" asked Alok, looking at the brothel owner expectantly.

"Here," she said, handing him two rupees.

"*Arre, ye kam hai. 5 ki baat hui thi,*" Alok protested. (This is too less. We agreed for 5 rupees.)

"*Bhadwe, 5 tere ko du to chokri ko kitna du, aur mai kitna rakhu?*" jibed the woman. (You pimp, if I give 5 rupees to you,what will I give to the girl, and what will I keep for myself?)

"*Galat baat, 5 ki baat hui thi, toh 5 do,*" said Alok with resilience. (That's wrong. Since we agreed on 5, you'll have to give me 5.)

"*Kya dimaag ki khol raha hai, ye le 3 rupaya.Aage nahi bol.*" (Why are you screwing my brain, take 3 rupees and don't ask for more.)

"*Thik hai…ab aap kehati ho to letahu…*" conceded Alok and took the money from her. (Fine. I will take it if you insist.)

The brothel owner then turned to Dagdu and instructed him to go inside, select the girl of his choice, and proceed. He nodded and went inside. Alok called after him and told him to come to his factory after he was done, and that they could go back home together in the morning. Dagdu replied okay and proceeded inside to select his girl, while Alok left for the factory.

The girl led Dagdu inside a room which contained a small bed and a table on which was placed a jar of water.

"*Chal, kaam chalu kar, utar kapade,*" said the sex-worker to him. (Come, remove your clothes and start your work.)

"*Han. Tera naam kya hai?*" (Okay, what's your name?)

"*Ye chutiya, shaadi banana ka hai mere se jo naam puch raha hai?*" (You rascal, are you here to get married to me that you are asking my name?)

"No."

"*Phir nalli saaf karne aaya hai, saaf kar aur nikal.Tere ko mai khush karungi.*" (You have come to release yourself. Do it and leave. I will give you pleasure.)

"*Mai aage piche dono.*" (I need your ass and cunt both.)

"*Kyaa abe, tu gandu hai…Piche nahi, sirf aage.*" (What, you asshole?No ass, only cunt.)

"*Paisa diya maine raat ka.*" (I have paid for the night.)

"*Haan to?*"(So what?)

"*Mere ko dono side mangta?*" (I need both sides.)

"Y*e dimag ki dahi mat kar.Sirf aage se matlab aage se, nahi to paisa vapas le aur nikal, bhainchod…*" (Listen, don't irritate me. I said no ass, means no ass.Else take your money and get lost, you sister fucker.)

"N*ako, nako, mai sirf aage se karunga.*"(No,no, I will only screw your cunt.)

The sex worker lay down on the bed, unclothed herself and said,"*Chal batti bujhaa aur aaja, time khoti mat kar.*"(Now switch off the lights and come on, don't waste time.)

Dagdu switches off the lights and undresses himself.He jumps on the woman and starts screwing her.

He got so carried away while screwing her that at one point, he forcefully turned her around and attempted a dog shot.She started screaming, "*Madarchod, tujhe bola piche se nahi,*" (Motherfucker, I told you no ass) but she could not overcome Dagdu's force. He became violent in the heat of passion and went on screwing her from the back.After sometime, both lay unclothed on the bed.

She was tired and screaming, "*Kutreyaa.*" (You dog.)

Dagdu just laughed at her and said,"*Mujhe bahot maza aaya.*" (I enjoyed a lot.) He then got up, got dressed and walked out of the room to head for the factory where Alok was on duty. The sex worker was still lying in bed in pain.

Alok asked Dagdu, "*Aur, maza aaya?*" (So, did you enjoy?)

"*Hmm, mast,*" replied Dagdu. (It was nice.)

"*Thik hai, mera commission de - do rupaya.*" (Alright then, give me my commission of 2 rupees.)

"*Kaheka commission?Raat me mila to tere ko.*" (Commission for what?You got your share last night.)

"*Madarchod, tere se bhi commission chaiye.*" (Motherfucker, I need a commission from you as well.)

"*Abhi nahi…kal deta hu,*" replied Dagdu. (Not now, I will give tomorrow.)

Alok put his hand into Dagdu's shirt pocket and dug out two rupees. He said, "*Bhaag madarchod yaha se. Thoda so le, subah nikalte hain…*" (Get lost, you motherfucker.Let's have some sleep now.We'll leave in the morning…)

At 8 AM the next morning, both of them left Bhiwandi. Dagdu escaped work at the hospital that day.

It was the second week of February, heralding in theseason of spring. Aadil was waiting at the coffee shop near the bus stop at 10 AM in the morning for that one special bus to arrive. He was smoking a cigarette, eagerly looking left and right. He looked at his wrist watch once and finally spotted the bus that he had been waiting for so eagerly. It came to a halt and multiple people got off and got on, while Aadil's eyes remained searching for her, but she wasn't there. He grew sad and irritated, thinking to himself that the day he had decided to talk to her about something important, she was nowhere to be seen. "She didn't take this bus today. Even yesterday, she wasn't in it. I don't understand this girl," he mumbled to himself. "Perhaps she took the next bus. I'll wait here for some more time."

Behind him, the hotel manager looked at him and smiled. He had a fair idea of whom Adil was waiting for, but feigned ignorance. His radio was on as usual. "Sa'ab, who are you waiting for?" he asked Aadil.

"No, for nobody," he replied, looking at the manager, then turned back to look at the bus that had just arrived.

"Oh Sa'ab, if you are not waiting for anybody, why are you so restless? Don't you want your daily cup of coffee today?"

Aadil looked at the manager irritatedly and said, "Why are you so bothered by it? Mind your own business." He looked at his wrist watch again and muttered, "Enough now, it's getting late." Another bus arrived just then and he restrained himself from leaving. He concluded that Amrita was going to be late.

Meanwhile, Amrita appeared at the coffee shop counter and said to the manager, "One coffee."

"4 aane," he replied.

Amrita handed him 50paise and took the balance of four aana back from him.

Aadillooked closely at the people descending from the bus and grew disappointed when he could not spot Amrita among them. He looked at his wrist watch again.

"It's 10:20," Amrita said from behind him.

Aadil jumped at the sound of her voice and turned around. He looked at her astonished.

"Let's go," she said and moved ahead. Aadil followed her wordlessly. Amrita finally broke the silence after they had walked quite some distance.

"It feels like two mute people are walking together," complained Amrita.

"Um…ha!Good morning, how are you?" Aadil asked nervously.

"Morning to you too. I am fine," she humoured him.

"I was just waiting like that," confessed Aadil.

"Ahan, I know."

As they reached the hospital gate, Aadil thought to himself, 'Boss, if you don't say it right now, you'll never be able to gather the courage to say it later.'

"Amrita, will you marry me?" he blurted out.

"What?" Amrita asked, still in a mocking disbelief.

"Noo…don't respond now. Think over it and give me an answer in the evening at Haji Ali. I will meet you there at 7 PM. I go there every Friday and it is Friday today," he pleaded innocently.

Amrita simply looked at him.

"I will wait for you there. I would have accompanied you, but Nafisa and Pritha are always with you."

Amritalaughed at him innocently and walked away, while Aadil remained standing there.

Ana Fernandes met Amrita at the entrance of the corridor and handed over a wedding card to her.

"Amrita, I'm getting married. Here's an invitation card for the wedding," she said happily.

Amrita shook her hand and said, "Wow, congratulations! When is it?"

"In 21 days,please do come."

"Of course, I will come," said Amrita and hugged Ana.

"Bring Aadil with you too."

"Have you invited him?"

"I am going to invite all.Pritha, Nafisa…but I am yet to hand them the card."

"Alright, take your time."

"I need to finish it all today itself, since I am on leave from tomorrow until the wedding."

Amrita smiled at her and said, "Okay, I'll leave you to it then. Bye." As she started to walk away, Ana called after her. Amrita stopped and turned. Ana walked up to her and said, "Don't forget to invite me at your own wedding."

"Ofcourse," said Amrita. "I would hate it if you don't come."

Ana smiled at her and walked away, while Amrita proceeded towards her office.

Later that day, Aadil lit a cigarette as he waited for Amrita at Haji Ali at 7 PM. Mumbai traffic was as bas as usual with people rushing to reach their destination. A bus came to a stop at Haji Ali junction, and Amrita got down amidst the crowd getting down and getting in. She spotted Aadil waiting for her and proceeded towards him.

"I hope I am not late," she said as she reached him.

"No," he responded softly.

"This place looks so nice," she said looking around.

"Yes, I come here quite regularly."

"You must be very religious."

"I am just human. Forget that, don't you know why I have called you here?" he asked with suppressed excitement.

Amrita pretended to be ignorant and said, "How would I know?"

"Have you thought about what I asked you in the morning? Will you marry me?" he asked again.

Amrita took a pause, then said, "Aadil, even if I say yes, do you think it will be possible for us to get married?"

"I just want to know what you want," insisted Aadil.

"Still…"

Both of them started walking. Aadil broke the brief silence and said, "Amrita, I am not forcing you for anything. We are best friends and will remain so despite whatever you decide."

Amrita gave Aadil her hand and leaned into his shoulder. Their eyes met. Aadil felt joyous and looked up at the sky, saying, "Bless us."

Amrita continued to look at Aadil and said, "Ana is getting married."

"I know, she has invited me," said Aadil, returning his gaze to her.

"They're both so lucky, they love each other."

"Yes and so am I," said Aadil in a pleased tone.

"How is that?" asked Amrita.

"Because I know I have your love," whispered Aadil while looking into Amrita's eyes.

Amrita smiled at him and said, "Nawab and Ashika have returned to Bombay.Let's go meet them."

"No, leave them alone. It's our time right now."

Both of them walked hand in hand from one end of the *dargah*to the other. Late evening, they took a taxi and reached Aadil's apartment at Prabhadevi where Amrita cooked dinner for both of them. After wrapping up the meal, Aadil turned on the radio and the song '*Kabhi Kabhi Mere Dil Me, Khayal Aata Hai, Ke Jaise Tujhko Banaya Gaya Hai Mere Liye*' was on. It was a song by Sahir Ludhiyanvi from the film 'Kabhi Kabhi' that was about to get released on 27th February.It was by pure coincidencethat the song which he had written for his beloved Amrita Pritam (thefamous Punjabi writer) was on when Aadil was at his house with Amrita by his side. Shyly and hesitantly, both of them drew closer and closer till they had each other in their arms.

At the hospital the next morning, Amrita and Aadil enteredtogether. Dagdu saw them as he was standing in one corner of the hospital compound near the entrance. He took out a bottle of alcohol and gulped down big swigs from it.He was drunk. When Amrita saw him, she commanded, "What are you doing there?"while Aadil stood nearby.

"*Kuch nahi, bus aise hi*," replied Dagdu. (Nothing, no reason.)

"Come," ordered Amrita, and Dagdu followed. They headed towards their department, while Aadil left for his department after saying goodbye to Amrita.

"Madam," said Dagdu.

"What is it?" Amrita asked.

"*Kuch paise do na.*" (Please give me some money.)

"*Kitne chahiye*?" asked Amrita. (How much do you need?)

"One rupee."

Amrita took out some money from her purse and gave it to Dagdu. Dagdu took it and said, "*Madam, pagar milte hi lauta dunga.*" (Madam, I will return it as soon as I get my salary.)

"*Ye ek chanta lagaungi na to thik ho jayega. Maine kaha vapas karane ko*?" said Amrita and playfully ruffled his hair. (You will get a tight slap from me, then you'll be fine.Did I askyou to return the money?)

Amrita and Aadil visited Siddhivinayak temple later that day to pray before lord Ganesha. Though muslim, Aadil didn't mind going to the temple to pray.After the prayer got over, he held Amrita's hand and said, "Did you know, the vein from this finger goes straight tothe heart?"

Amrita shook her head and looked into Aadil's eyes. He took out a ring from his pocket and said, "Listen, I want to put this ring on your finger."

Amrita giggled and said, "Go ahead."

Aadil slid the ring over her ring finger and they both walked out of the temple together.

Outside the temple, Amrita sawan astrologer siting with a few people surrounding him. She turned to Aadil and said, "Let's go see that astrologer."

"Amrita…do you really believe in all this?" Aadil asked and chuckled.

"Come na…" insisted Amrita and pulled Aadil by the hand towards the astrologer.

"Baba, look at our hands," said Amrita upon reaching him.

"Ofcourse," said the astrologer and made them sit in front of him. He started examining the lines of their hands, simultaneously asking them about their dates of birth, time and place. He then looked at Aadil and said, "My child, you are so lucky." He gestured at Amrita and said, "You will marry this girl and have a prosperous and happy married life."

Amritagiggled and exclaimed, "Really?"

"My predictions are never wrong," claimed the astrologer while looking at the sky. "God has created both of you for each other."

Amrita and Aadil left his company and headed over to Shivaji Park next to thesea shore.

Aadil turned to Amrita and asked, "Had the astrologer said that we could never get married, what would you have done?"

"I would have broken his jaw. And listen, don't you dare say this ever again," she replied.

"Why?"

"Because if our marriage doesn't happen, then…"

"Then, what?"

"I shall never talk to you for the rest of my life."

"Hey! hey Amrita, I was only kidding," appeased Aadil, trying to put an arm around a resisting Amrita.

"I don't like such jokes."

"Okay, I won't say it again. Please, smile now."

Amrita stopped resisting and smiled.

AnaFernandes got married a few days before the festival of Holi and everyone from the hospital graced the occasion. A special celebration for Holi was planned at Rhuhi's house.

Bhaucha Dhakka or Ferry Wharf in Bombaywas well known for its fish market. Many fish vendors, both male and female, thronged there early in the morning to purchase fish on a whole-sale rate, then proceededto supply or sell them off in the local market.

On the day of Holi, 16th March 1976, Nawab and Ashika went there early in the morning to buy Pomfret for Amrita. Since she was Bengali,she was fond of fish and Pomfret was her favourite. From Ferry Wharf,they were to head straight to Ashika's flat in Worli which she was still occupying after marriage. They regularly shuffled between Noorani Mazil in Nagpada and the house in Worli depending upon their work schedule and convenience. Nawab had decided to move in with Ashika at her Worli abode in April.Ashika bargained with a fisherwoman and boughta kilogram of white pomfret.

They were just about to leave the place when a maroon coloured Premier Padmini came to a screeching halt a few meters away and a few notorious looking menstepped out withchopper swords and pistols. They moved about as if desperately searching for someone. As soon as they entered the market, the people there broke into a frenzy in anticipation of a crime likely to be committed. No one had the audacity to even look at these people in the eye.Fishermen and women started running about to save their lives.

Feeling clueless, Nawab simply looked on, stunned and surprised. Some of these men headed straight for where Nawab stood with Ashika, holding her hand tightly. A man, no very far from them, took the hit of a bullet while trying to run away from the scene and fell at Nawab's feet. Nawab felt afraid, not for his own life, but for his love, Ashika. He couldn't imagine letting anything happen to her. He was about to rush away with her when a goon dashed past Ashika and knocked her unintentionally to one side. As if by reflex, Nawab shouted,"Bastard, can't you see?"

"Come again? What did you say?" challenged the goon.

Terrified out of her wits, Ashika tried to control Nawab's anger and said, "Leave it, Nawab."

Nawab didn't react as he wanted to avoid a confrontation. He kept his calm this time and turned to walk away. The goon became more audacious by this response. He followed after Ashika and tried to touch her, saying, "What will you do?"

Losing his temper, Nawab lost control of himself, picked up a sharp sickle from a fish containerand brought it down over the goon's arms, chopping away the very hand with which he had dared to touch Ashika.The goon fell unconscious. Nawab didn't know how to react to what he had just done and dropped the sharp weapon in his hands. Ashika fainted at the sight of so much blood shed.

The rest of the goons were continuously firing and stabbing at targets who seemed to be from the rival gang. Nawab wasn't aware of anything until he turned around and saw the bloodshed, the dead bodies and the scattered fish. The black tar road of Bhaucha Dhakka was running with red. It was a red Holi with killing,shootouts and blood everywhere. Nawab was trying to pull an unconscious Ashika up in his arms when suddenly he saw a man running towards him with a sword. He panicked,picked up the same sickle as before and swung it in his direction with full force. The sicklebeheaded that man and his body and severed head plopped to the ground. Another man came running up to Nawab, pulled him aside and said, "Run away from here, go! Take that car," while pointing at at the maroon Premier Padmini.

Nawab pulled Ashika up in his arms and ran towards the car. The man followed after them and got into the car with them. He then shouted out to the goons who who had come to conduct the massacre,"Run away, the job is done."

That Premier Padmini sped away from Dhakka towards an unknown destination. Later on, Nawab learned that the man who had escorted them to thecarwas none other than Barkat Ali, a well known gold smuggler. "Thank you for saving my life," said Barkat,revealing further that the sword man's main target had in fact been him, not Nawab. The car dashed towards the Radio Club in Colaba.Right opposite to it was Barkat Ali's guest house. He kept Nawab and Ashika in his safe custody.

Around noon, Aadil pickedAmrita up from her hostel and they proceeded towards Ashika's Worli house together.

They reached in another half an hour, only to find the door of her apartment locked from the outside. They waited there for another hour, then approached the neighbours and the security guard outside to seek information on their whereabouts. Upon enquiry, the security guard told them that they had left the house early in the morning, but hadn't returned yet. Aadil and Amrita now felt worried. After waiting for some more time, they left Worli for their respective abodes. Aadil wished Amrita happy holi and dropped her offat her hostel before leaving for his house inMatunga.

At Barkat Ali's guest house, Nawab andAshika were being treated as guests, but their minds were still occupied by the incidents from that morning. Both were shocked and worried about their future. "What will I say to *di*?"Nawab asked Ashika. Ashika didn't answer,but started crying instead. Nawab consoled her. They spent a very anxious time there till evening.

Barkat entered the guest house later that day along with a few goons and the same chap whose hand had been chopped off by Nawab. He and Ashika got up and pleaded him to let them go. Barkat smiled and said,"Trust me, nothing will happen to you.Please take your seat."They took the seats in one corner, while Barkat took the one in the middle. The other people in the room remained standing. "Salim, come here," commandedBarkat, gesturing at the man with chopped hands to come forwards.

Salim drew closer to them and said while pointing at Nawab,"*Mujhe isko tapkane ka hai!*" (I want to kill him!)

"You will do nothing of that sort," warned Barkat while staring at Salim.

Still adamant, Salim pulled out his gun with his other hand and aimed it at Nawab, his finger ready at the trigger. He shouted,"*Barkat bhai, mujhe kuch nahi sunna hai.Isko mai khallas karega.*" (Barkat bhai, I don't know anything. I just want to kill him.)

Barkat got up to stand infront of Salim and yelled, "*Chala goli. Apne dhande ka usool hai,zubaan diya to diya. Isne apoon ka jaan bachaya, maine isko jubaan diya kuch nahi hoga, phir tu mujhe goli maar aur bhadas nikal.*" (Shoot!It's the principle of our business, I stand by my word. He saved my life and I gave him my word that I will not let anything happen to him. Shoot me, thus, and release your anger.)

Nawab andAshika sat shivering, scared for their lives. Salim dropped his gun and hugged Barkat.Barkat pattedSalim's back and told him, "*Tu iski begum ko haath nahi lagata to aisa kuch nahi hota.Apan log sone ka smuggling karte hai, ye aurat baazi nahi.*" (If you had not touched his wife, nothing of this sort would have happened.Wedo business in gold smuggling, not womanising.)

He then called on Nawab to come forward and asked the two of them to hug each other and apologise. Nawab bowed in front of Salim with folded handsand said, "*Ashika meri jaan hai.Aap usko galat tarike se chhune wale the, bhai, anjaane me ho gayi galati ghusse me.*"(Ashika is my life. You were about to touch her inappropriately, and the mishap happened unknowingly in that moment of anger.)

"Come on,Salim.Forgive him now," instructed Barkat while looking at both of them. Salim's chopped hand had been dressed in a bandage. He pulledNawab to his chest with another hand and said,"Since bhai has commanded it, I will forgive you."

Barkat called for tea and snacks, and everyone took a seat.He further asked Nawab to relax and offered for Ashika to be sent to rest in a bedroom on the first floor. Nawab agreed to it and Ashika was escorted away.

"You will work for us from now on," Barkat told Nawab.

"What's the work?" asked Nawab.

"You went to Dhaka to get fish, didn't you? We will give you a gold fish, but to take the parcel of my gold fish, you'll have to go yourself.Salim will explainthe rest to you," said Barkat and instructedSalim to explain everything to Nawab.

Nawab asked further,"How much money will I get?" "The amount that you earn in a month, you'll receive in a day per container," replied Barkat.

Nawab simply kept quiet thereafter.While Salim explained the tricks of the trade to him, he realized that gold fish was nothing but a code word for gold smuggling. Everyone left after tea and snacks. Before leaving, Barkat said to Nawab, "You take rest, and if you need anything, just tell the security."

"Alright," answered nawab.

Barkat had political backing that went all the way up to Delhi.Hence,he managed to tone down the morning massacreand blood-shed at Dhakkathough his channels overnight before print media could report it and blow his identity out. In any case, it was the time of emergency, so print media editors were no better than political puppets. The nextmorning, the incident was coloured and presented as'Holi confrontations chaos' and the stampede that had lead to two accidental deaths were reported, burying the actual incident.This cover-up was cooked up in the night to serve on the breakfast tables of the people of Bombay.

Two days later, Nawab was dropped off at his hospital by Barkat Ali's personal vehicle.When he met Amrita, he told her all about the holi mischief and Barkat Ali's job proposal. He further asked to be relived from his job at the hospital. Amrita reasoned with him, saying that the path chosen by him was not right, but if he had decided, they all only wished the best for him. In those days, no strict notice period policy was followed by most organisations, hence at Nawab's request, Amrita managed to convince the hospital management to relieve him in a week's time.

For all ofthe next week, Nawab completed all his pending assignments. His affection and respect for Amrita and Aadil hadn't changed. He knew that he was taking the wrong step under his greed for money, but he felt quite trapped and compelled to do this in the situation. After a week, he left the hospital with tears in his eyes and a promise to his beloved sister Amrita and the rest of his hospital friends that he would keep in touch and seek their blessings as always.

Nafisa, who had been standing in one corner, came up to Nawab and said,"Khan *sahib*, you are a kind-hearted person. I only joked around with you before.If any of my actions have been to your displeasure, please forgive me.*Allah hafiz*."

Nawab smiled and said,"Thanks, I shall keep visiting to meet you all. I have only left this job, not the city."

Aadil hugged him goodbye. "Brother, take good care of Ashika,"saidAmrita with a choked voice. Nawab nodded and said a tearful goodbye to all of them. He shook hands with Dr.Randhawa andDr. Wadia before leaving through the hospitalgates once and for all.Back home, Nawab told Ashika to take medical leave from Dr.Awasthi's Hospital for her pregnancy.

For the next six months, Nawab put in all his hard-work and energy intoBarkat's venture and mastered the art of business. In the meantime, he had also left Noorani Manzil, his flat in Nagpada, and had moved in with Ashika at her Worli flat. Occasionally, he would take some time out to meet Amrita and Aadil inWorli or at Aadil's place. In theprevious six months, Nawab had earned reputation and goodwill in Barkat's eyes as well as his team's. In fact, Barkat treated Nawab as the next in command and was the de facto in-charge of the operation. By this time, Nawab had made a fortune too.

Ashikadelivered a baby boy on September 28th, 1976 and they named him Asman. Nawab and Ashika planned a party to celebrate the new arrival in their family for 12th October, 1976. Barkat willingly agreed to give his guest house at Radio Club as the venue for this party. Nawab invited all his hospital friends, Amrita and Aadil included.

On 12th October, 1976,it happened so that Barkat had to travel to Madras urgently to meet with ajewellerbusinessman Jagan Mohan Joshi in Coimbatore.He boardedthe Indian Airlines 171at Santa Cruz Airport in Bombay at 1:35 PM. While taking off, however,the plane crashed, causing the death of various passengers, Barkat being one amongst them.

News spread by that evening and the birthday celebration was cancelled.Instead,a discussion over who was going to be Barkat's successor starting taking form.Unanimously, Nawabwas chosen as the new Chief, but there was one manwithin the group who wasn't happy with Nawab promotion.It was Salim, but he pretended otherwise.

The next morning, Barkat's dead body was buried at*Bada Kabrasthan*in Chandanwadi where the who's who of Bombay mafia graced the occasion to pay their last tributes to the departed soul. Nawab led the proceedings since he was now the new Chief of Barkat's enterprise. Back home, he asked Ashika not to resume her job at Dr.Awasthi's Hospital post the delivery of their son.At the hospital, Amrita entered her department one morning to find Dagducrouching in one corner. As soon as he saw her, he shuffled about hurriedly and tried to hide something behind his back.

"What are you hiding?" Amrita asked sternly.

"N…nn…nothing," said Dagdu, his voice slurring.

Amrita could by now smell the odour of a spirit. "I smell something foul in this room."

"What are you talking about?" he asked nervously.

"I think it is alcohol. Are you drinking here?" she asked and started walking towards Dagdu. "Show me, what are you hiding?"

"It's nothing."

Amrita tried to catch hold of Dagdu, while he resisted. The bottle of alcohol slipped from his hands and tumbled down to the floor. Amrita bent forward to pick up the bottle, but her sari was not appropriately in place, exposing a good part of her chest to him.Amrita picked up the bottle, whileDagdu kept looking at her breasts, stunned. She got up and adjusted her sari in place, ignorant ofDagdu's silent gaze fixed on her chest.

"I have been observing you for the past few days, your mind is not in your work," reprimanded Amrita. Dagdu remained quiet. Amrita grew irritated and yelled, "Why don't you speak? Are you dumb? I shall complain to Dr. Randhawa about you."

"Madam, I won't ever repeat it again. I swear to you. I am sorry," pleaded Dagdu.

Amrita simply stared at him, threw the bottle away and left the room. Dagdu rushed to the washroom soon after she was gone and masturbated.

Two weeks later, Sanjay Gandhi,the powerful young son of the then prime minister Indira Gandhi was to visit Mumbai.He was already (in)famous for having implementedthe sterilisation programme and for the demolition of Turkman gate inDelhi in April of the same year. He was an uncrowned king during the emergency.With the blessings of the ruling establishment, the massacres and the rioting were not even reported, and the Turkman gate massacre was no exception.Such was the authority and fear he commanded that the entire establishment toed to his wishes during his visit. Bombay was on a standstill.At the age of only 29, Sanjay Gandhi was the de facto prime minister of India.

Diwali was approaching and Amrita, Aadil,Nafisa, together with Nawab, Ashika and their new born son Asman celebrated the festival together. From November 10th to 15th of 1976, the first cricket match of the New Zealand-India tour was to be held at Wankhede Stadium. Using his influential connections, Nawabhad managed to get tickets for all his friends from the hospital, including Dr. Randhawa, Dr. Wadia, Aadil, Amrita, Nafisa,Pritha,and even Dagdu. After the match got over, they all gathered together insideGarware Club at the stadium where a surprise announcement was to be made by Aadil. He announced to everyone his wish to marry Amrita and came forward with a ring to put onAmrita's third finger of her left hand. Everyone cheered loudly and congratulated them. Swept by emotion, Nawab and Ashika announced a grand party for the couple on the day of their engagement on 28th November.

On Friday, 26th November, Dagdu'seyes shone like an owl's with anger in them. He was thinking about Amrita, looking at her waist through her white sari.His gaze travelledin an upward direction and stopped at her breasts. He wanted to bite her lips.He wanted to trap her, so was waiting for her to come and be trapped. She was about to enter her department after finishing her day's tasks at the hospital.

Outside,the city of Mumbai was washed in the golden light of a mellow sunset as usual. Even the sea was coloured scarlet and golden with the drowning sun. Traffic was at its peak on Mumbai roads with a sea of people in best buses, cars, taxies, or local trains, heading towards theirrespective homes or other destinations before nightfall.

The door of Amrita's cabin lay open. When she saw it on her way out, she felt slightly suspicious. By that time, most of her fellow colleagues including Nafisa,Aadil, Dr.Randhawa and Dr. Wadia had left the hospital for the day. She decided to quickly check what was amiss.

"Who has left this door open? Nobody is serious with their work anymore," she muttered as she made her way to the room. "Is there anyone here?" she asked as she entered the room and looked around. "I guess there is noone inside. I am bothering about it unnecessarily." She bolted the door from inside, deposited her bag over her table, took a bunch of keys out of it and went over to her almirah. She then opened the almirah and took out from it a neatly folded blue sari. She proceeded to remove the apron and the white sari that she had on, kept these clothes on the table next to her purse, and started to put on the blue sari that she had just taken out of the almirah. It was Aadil's favourite and she wanted to surprise him by meeting him in that outfit before he left for the day. She wasn't aware, however, that he had left already.

While she was taking out her sari, a wooden rod had fallen out of the almirah, but had escaped her notice. Though when she started to put on her blue sari, she saw it and bent down to pick it up. Just then, he heard somebody jump right behind her. She turned around alarmed and was shocked to see Dagdu there. He had been hiding on themezzanine floor, waiting for her.

"*Tum…tum yahan kya kar rahe ho?*" she asked, growing pale. (You…what are you doing here?)

"*Abhi tak toh maine kuch kiya nahi hai,*" he replied slyly. (I haven't done anything yet.)

"*Dekho, chale jao. Na…nahi to mai…*" (Look, just leave, or else I…)

Dagdu laughed. "*Ab kidhar gaya tera rubab, chinal?*" (Where has your arrogance gone now, you prostitute.) While speaking this, he pulled out his leather belt from his pants.

Scared numb, Amrita fell to her knees and folded her hands in front of him. "*Please, tum yahan se chale jao.*" (Please, leave this place.)

"*Bagair kuch kiye?*" he asked. (Without doing anything?) He tied the belt around herneck and twisted it.

Amrita felt a shooting pain around her neck before the sensation of choking set in. Her eyes popped out of their sockets and drool escaped her lips. She tried to speak through her choked throat, "*Please, mujhe chhor do…jane do.*" (Please, leave me. Let me go.)

Dagdu asked angrily, "*Itni jaldi, raand?*"(What's the hurry, you slut?)

He continued pulling at her by the belt around her neck, while Amrita struggled to catch hold of Dagdu's hands with both of her own. She exerted all her energy and managed to pull Dagdu down to the floor, while getting up herself. Two buttons from her blouse had popped openduring this struggle, and her breast was exposed. She picked up the paperweight from her table and aimed it at Dagdu. It hit Dagdu's back.

"*Madarchod…tula shodnar nahi,*" he exclaimed as he felt the pain and tried to get up. (Motherfucker, I won't leave you.)

"You fucking bastard!" screamed Amrita angrily and kickedDagdu between his legs with all her energy, then ran towards the door.

"*Aai ga!*" Dagdu cried in pain and fell back to his side. He looked around desperately and found the paper weightlying right next to him. He managed to pick it up with one hand, the other pressed firmly over his crotch,and launched it at Amrita.

She had reached the door and was fidgeting with the bolt when the paper weight hit her head and she fell down with a moan adjacent to the door. She lay face down on the floor, semi-conscious.

Dagdu got up and pulled her back by the leather belt still tied around her neck, saying, "*Aai ghali, tera ko chorega nahi mai.*" (You motherfucker, I won't leave you now.)

With whatever energy Amrita had left in her body, she raised herself up and bit Dagdu atvarious places on his body in an attempt tofree herself. "You rascal!" she gasped.

Dagdu evaded Amrita's bites as far as he could and tightened the leather belt around her neck. Holding her down, he tied both her hands behind her back with the loose end of the belt, then pushed her towards the table. "*Sali kutri!*" (Bloody bitch!) He walked upto her and tore open her blouse. Her white bra now became visible underneath. Her chest was heaving from the short gasps of breath that she was struggling to take in. Dagdu removed her petticoat next.He white coloured pantiesseemeddirty and wet, soaked in bad-smelling blood. He tried to pull it down, while Amrita tried her best to kick him off.

Dagdu unleashed a string of expletives at her as he fell on his back near the window. With her panties, a soiled sanitary napkin had come away in his hand. The smell made him nauseous."*Chinal sali, tere ko aaj hi ke din ye hone ko tha?*" (You slut, did you have to get this today only?)

He got up,threw the napkin to one side and looked out the window. The sight of a dog sniffing the rear of another female dog made his eyes sparkle. A notorious idea had taken birth in his mind. He rushed towards the table where Amrita was lying on her back, pulled her up by the ankles and turned her over. While she lay on her stomach in front of him, naked and exposed, he pushed open the chain of his pants, lowered himself down to his knees and engaged in the inhuman act of sodomy.

Upon releasing himself in her,he pulled up his pants and said,"*Saali, agar age ka nahi mila to apun ko piche ka bhi chalta hai.*" (Bitch, if I can't get your cunt, I am okay with your ass too.)

Breathing heavily, he went to stand next to the window. When he spotted the soiled napkin lying under it, he picked it up and keptit in his pocket.Outside, both the dogs had finished their work too. He took out a Shivaji bidi from his pocket, placed it in between his lips and lit it with a match. He then looked at Amrita, threw the matchstick out the window, not realizing that the wrapper of hisShivajibidi packet had also fallen by the window.He took a deep puff of the bidi and exhaled the white smoke out the window.It was now dark outside and the city of Mumbai carried on as usual.

After finishing his bidi, he turned around and saw a wooden rod lying to one side of the almirah.He picked it up and inserted it forcefully into her anus. He then tore apart a portion of her apron,stuffed it in her mouth and tied it up around her head so that she would not scream.

At 10 AM the next morning, Aadil waited for Amrita at the café house near the Worli bust stop 15 minutes away from the hospital as usual. They had made it a ritual to have coffee there together before going to work. Aadil kept waiting in eager anticipation, but she did not turn up. Finally growing desperate after looking at his wrist watch multiple times, he asked the café shop manager, "Has that madam left already?"

"No sir, she never leaves without you," he replied.

Aadil kept waiting at the cafe till 11 AM, hoping to see her in every bus that came to a stop there.Eventually, he told the café manger,"Sir, if madam comes, ask her to meet me at the hospital."

"Alright sir, but won't you have your coffee?" asked the manager.

"Later," he said and rushed towards the hospital.

As soon as she reached the OPD department right next to the hospital's entrance, sister Surekha Patil approached him and said, "Aadil. there is a problem."

"What happened?" Aadil asked hesitantly.

"Amrita…Amrita…" she stuttered in response.

"What happened to her?" he asked alarmed.

"There was an attempt to murder."

"What?" Aadil was in disbelief."Where is she?"

"In the emergency room…"

Aadil thanked her and rushed towards the emergency room. When he reached there, he saw Dr. Jagmohan Randhawacoming out of the room. He looked at Aadil and said, "Come with me."

"Dr. Randhawa, what happened to Amrita?Is she okay?" asked Aadil frantically, while walking beside him.

"It's bad,Dr. Aadil," he replied in a grim and upset voice.

“What do you mean,doctor?”

They now entered Dr. Randhawa’s cabin. He took his chair behind his desk and said, “It doesn’t look good,doctor.Actually, it’s quite bad.”

Aadil took a chair too and asked, “Doctor, are the injuries only external?”

“I wish it was only external…I am not sure.We are awaiting a medical report from Dr. Wadia. It’s an emergency. I think I should inform the police first,” said Dr. Randhawa and picked up the receiver of the phone on his table. He dialled and waited for a few seconds before saying, “Hello, police? A…one second.” He then looked at Aadil and said, “Please, excuse me.”

Panicking, Aadil left his office to go back to the emergency room. Dr.Randhawa, on the other hand, connected back on line and said,“Hello sir, I am Dr. Jagmohan Randhawa, dean of Verma Memorial Hospital.There has been an attempt to murder and robbery of a lady doctor hereat the hospital.”

In the corridor, Nafisa and Pritha wereworriedly discussing the same. They had been unaware of the incident, but on persistent enquiry with the nurses on duty, they learned that Amrita had been raped and sodomised. Aadil was shocked and angry upon hearing the truth and desperately wanted to know who the culprit was, but nobody knew who had done it. Nafisa was in tears herself, but tried to console Aadil who looked quite disturbed,angry, devastated and shocked with the news of such a heinous crime committed against his beloved.

A police van entered the gates of the hospital, and S.I. Mr. Arun Jogalekar along with two lady constables, a male constable and a photographer accompanied Dr. Jagmohan

Randhawa to the crime scene. Aadil and his colleagues followed after them too. S.I. Jogalekar took stock of the situation and asked the constables to inspect each and every minute detail of the crime scene. He also enquired with the hospital staff about the details of the victim, and if they suspected anyone who could have committed the crime. The hospital staff co-operated with them, but they were clueless on the culprit themselves. The photographer tookpictures of the crime scene and the victim. While searching throughthe crime scene, a constable foundthe half-burned Shivaji bidi and its wrapper. He picked them up for evidence. Blood samples and fingerprints were also taken by the forensics team. S.I. Joglekar asked Dr.Randhawa and Dr.Wadia to submitthe medical report as soon as possible.

Amrita was transferred from the emergency ward tothe I.C.U. Officer Joglekar took statements from all the staff members and prepared a statement. Upon the completion of the initial enquiry, he left the hospital with his team. Back at the police station, they took cognisance of the crime and started further investigation to hunt down the culprit.

Still unaware of all that had transpired, Nawab and Ashika were busy preparing for the party on the evening of 28th November. Ashika was flipping through the newspaper while having tea that morning when she learned about the incident and informed Nawab about it. Nawab wasshocked and angry beyond measure and immediately rushed to the hospital with Ashika. The party which he had been planning for Amrita and Aadil's engagement was naturally cancelled.They met Aadil as soon as they reached the hospital and were led by him to the ward where Amrita lay unconscious. Nawab cried uncontrollably at the sight of his beloved sister in that condition, while Ashika and Aadil tried to console him with tears in their own eyes.

Dr. Wadia got a call from the police station, reminding him toturn in Amrita's medical report. As soon as it was ready, Dr.Randhawa deputeda ward boy to carry the report in a sealed envelope to the police station where it was forwarded to S.I.Joglekar. As per the report, Amrita had been sodomised. S.I. Joglekar deputed a constable to enquire who all at the Hospitalwere bidi smokers, particularly Shivaji bidi, and ordered him to make a list of their names. Through this exercise, Dagdu's name surfaced.He was a habitual bidi smoker, and according to one of the hospital ward boys,he used to smoke Shivaji bidi exclusively. Nafisa and Aadil also confirmed to the police constable that Dagdu indeed used to smoke bidi.

At 9:30 PM that night, Aadil was sitting on a bench outside Amrita's room. He checked his pockets in search of a cigarette, but there was none. He pulled out his wallet, took out some spare change from it and looked around. When a ward boy passed him by, he summoned him and requested him to go buy him aWills' cigarette. The ward boy nodded, took the money from him andwalked away.

Aadil got up to walk around a little bit in the meantime, then went into Amrita's room. Watchingher lying in bed in her state, he felt deep pain and hoped that she would wake up in twenty four hours, and perhaps name the rascal who had done this to her once she was conscious. The ward boy returned with his cigarette box. He patted the ward boy, took a cigarette out and kept the box in his pocket.

Opposite the door of her room, the corridor of the hospital extended into a little pillared balcony. He walked into it, took out a lighter and lit the cigarette between his lips. In that moment while he stood next to a pillar, he was transported back in his memory to a moment that he had shared with Amrita at the Radio Club hotel near Marine Lines.

“Aadil, cigarette smoking is injurious to health. It’s written on the packet,” Amrita had said.

“Leave it, yaar,” Aadil had replied mildly annoyed.

“Alright,” said Amrita and dropped the cigarettebox into the sea.

“What did you do?” exclaimed Aadil.

"You asked me to leave it, so I left it,” she replied with a mischievous smile.

“You behave just like a child sometimes. It’d be better if you have one instead.”

“Fine then. Give me a child right now.”

“Are you mad!?” exclaimed Aadil.

"For you,” said Amrita while leaning into his arms.

Aadil kissedAmrita and took her in his arms.

In an unconscious motion,he wrapped his arms around the pillar he was standing next to. The very next moment, Nawab patted him from behind and drew him out of his dream.

“How come you’re here this late at night? Ashika must be alone at home,” he asked Nawab.

“Don’t worry about Ashika.Come on, have some food.You haven’t eaten anything for two days. Let’s have dinner together. Ashika has prepared it,” Nawab insisted.

Aadil wasn’t in the mood to eat, but after great persuasion by Nawab, he agreed. After dinner, Nawab asked Aadil to go home and take rest till the next morning. He went along with him to his residence at Matunga, dropped him off and then leftfor his own house where Ashika was waiting for him.

At 8 AM the next morning, the manager of the coffee shop near the hospital was busy performing *pooja,* after which he switched on the radio kept on the counter and started reading the newspaper. A song from the movie 'Anand','*Jindagi, kaise hai paheli…*' came on. Inside his cafe, a few customers were having tea or coffee. Just then, a waiter came to inform him that they were running out of coffee powder and that they needed to order some to replenish their stock. He ask him to order it immediately from asupplier named Thambi, when suddenly his gaze fell upon the news regarding Amrita in the newspaper. Utterly shocked, he left everything under the supervision of that waiter, and rushed towards the hospital. He saw a huge crowd gathered near the gate. No one was allowed to go inside, but they were all whispering about Amrita. The manager stood helpless.

One amongst the crowd said, "If such things happen at the hospital, then only God can save us."

Another said, "I heard that it's a rape case!"

"Yeah, even I heard the same.It has been reported in the newspaper as well," joined in another.

"These hospital guys are hiding something."

"I heard that the girl was likely to marry some Dr. Aadil from the same hospital."

"How do you know that?"

"See, it's written here in the newspaper."

"Ohh, she was going to marry a muslim."

"What rubbish!" the manager exclaimed upon hearing all the talk in the crowd.

"We are only repeating what's written here in the newspaper," claimed the first guy.

"What right do you guys have to talk about someone else's personal life?" the manager asked angrily."Have any of you ever offered them any help or did favours for them in their bad times? For God's sake, stop all this nonsense.This is a terrible accident, and it has not happened in this city or in this country for the first time. What do you know about Amrita? If this could happen to her, it can happen to any of you too, or your sisters,mothers, or daughters.So please, stop it!"He left the place in anguish since he could not gain entry into the hospital anyway.

Inside the hospital, the trustees, Dr. Jagmohan Randhawa andDr.Wadia were conducting their meeting, discussing the issues and repercussions of Amrita's incident.

"What is the scene Dr. Jagmohan Randhawa? How could this happen at our hospital? Do you suspect anybody?" asked the Chairman.

"I wish I had a clue, sir," he replied.

"There have been no arrests till now," continued the Chairman. "Doctor, never before in this hospital's history has an incident like this taken place, that too with a lady doctor. The reputation of the hospital is in question. As theChairman of Verma Memorial Trust, I am answerable to our patrons, the people and the government." He then turned to Dr. Wadia and said, "Dr. Wadia, what do the medical reports suggest?I mean, how serious is the matter? Has she been raped?"

“Yes, but not that kind of a rape, sir,” replied Dr. Wadia.

“What do you mean? What other kind is there?” asked the Chairman perplexed.

“She has been sodomised, sir,” he replied.“A wooden rod was forced into her anus according to the gynaecologist. Her hymen is still intact. There has been no vaginal damage. I suspect that her carotid artery that carries blood to the brain has been damaged seriously. I feel she needs an immediate carotid angiography.”

“Please go ahead with it then,” said the Chairman. “Verma Memorial Trust takes responsibility for all her medical expenses till she recovers fully, and you shall have this in writing.”

“Sir, there is a problem,” interrupted Dr. Randhawa. “Medico-legally speaking,one needs a relative’s permission before going ahead with a carotid angiography on a patient, and she has none.”

"Then please find someone, doctor. There must be someone,” insisted the Chairman.

“Sorry sir, but there is none that I know of.”

Dr. Wadiainterrupted, “We could speak to Aadil about it. He is her would-be-husband after all.”

“Can we take permission from Aadil?” the Chairman asked Dr. Randhawa.

“No, Aadil was indeed going to marry her, but they had not associated officially.They are not married and he is not her husband yet.”

“Oh, I see. How far has the police reached?” asked the Chairman.

"They are still investigating. We have lodged a complaint for attempt to murder and robbery," replied Dr. Randhawa gravely.

"I feel sorry for Amrita, but I cannot jeopardise the interests of the hospital, particularly when I know that people will try to take advantage of an already critical situation of this poor girl,"said the Chairman with sadness in his voice.

Dr. Wadia and Nafisa entered into Amrita's room and started the regular round of checkups on her. He instructedNafisa to attend to some medical care, while he left the room to return to his chamber. He looked out of his window to see a police jeep entering the hospital premises.

S.I. Jogalekar got down from the police jeepalong with his team and marched towards the main corridor where he met Dr. Aadil and enquired him about Amrita's health.

"Still unconscious," he replied.

"And where is Dr.Randhawa?" he asked further.

"He must be in his cabin," answeredAadil.

"Alright, I will check with him," said S.I. Joglekar and turned to leave.

Suddenly,Nafisa came running towards Aadil and said, "There is good news,Aadil! Amrita is finally coming out of her unconscious state. I have seen it myself!"

On hearing this, S.I. Jogalekar stopped himself and stayed to listen to the entire conversation.

"Really!? Let's go in and see," exclaimed Aadiland both of them rushed towards Amrita's room.On the way, they informedDr. Wadia of it too and he joined them.

Amrita was slowly gaining consciousness and was trying to say something, but only unintelligible sounds escaped her lips.

“Amrita, say something…please,” said Aadil as soon as he reached her side.

Amrita opened her eyes to look at Nafisa, Dr. Wadia and then Aadil.Her eyeballs rotated twice or thrice, registering the faces of these people.

“Yes, my dear…please say something,” encouraged Dr. Wadia.

Aadil leaned in closer towards her face and looked into her eyes. “Amrita…” he whispered.

The moment their gazes met, Amrita suffered a spasticpost traumatic flashback and started screaming. Herloud cries sounded inhuman and she became rowdy and restless.

Aadil felt terrified of this sight ofhis beloved. He couldn't believe that Amrita had failed to recognise him, and kept murmuring, “Amrita…Amrita…”

Dr. Wadia instructed Nafisa to take Aadil away. He understood that his presence was stimulating a violently defensive reaction from her. In the meantime, S.I. Jogalekar and Dr. Randhawa arrived at the scene. Dr. Wadia and Aadil walked out of the I.C.U. together.

"Is she out of trouble?” asked Dr. Randhawa. Dr. Wadia simply looked at him wordlessly.

S.I. Jogalekar asked Dr. Randhawa, “Is she out of coma?”

“No,” Dr. Wadia almost screamed at S.I. Jogalekar. He then turned to Dr. Jagmohan Randhawa and said,“She needs an urgent carotid angiography.Please give me the permission for it. Aadil will sign all the papers, but for God's sake, please allow me to operate on her."

"I give you the permission to go ahead with the angiography," said Aadil desperately.

"My dear sir, please put yourself in my shoes. It's not possible legally," pleaded Dr. Randhawa.

"What is this fucking legal problem? Her life is more precious than any legality, doctor," exclaimed Aadil.

Dr. Wadia looked right at Dr. Randhawa and said, "Doctor, she has become too sensitive and hostile to male touch. You know that if an angiography is not done immediately, she won't be able to recoverher life."

"I am helpless," said Dr. Randhawa, then turned to S.I. Jogalekar. "Sorry sir, I cannot permit you to take her statement right now.Please understand the problem,"he said and turned to leave the place.

S.I. Jogalekar called after him, "Excuse me, Dr. Randhawa, you may not be able to give me permission for interrogation at this moment, but when she is stable and recovers from unconsciousness completely, kindly inform me."

"Oh, sure," he replied.

S.I. Jogalekar heaved a deep sigh and said, "Though I do want to take statements froma few more witnesses from the hospital right now."

"You have the power, inspector. Go ahead," said Dr. Randhawa and left.

S.I. Jogalekar did a round of questions with Aadil, the nurseSuman Patil, a ward boy, Pritha, Nafisa and Dagdu.

While questioning,Dagdu came across as very nervous, tense and afraid. S.I. Joglekar smelled something wrong, and when Dagdu left the interrogation room, S.I. Joglekar asked one of his constables to keep an eye on him. The constable obediently replied,"Yes, sir. I feel that he is the culprit too.Look how the mother fuckeris shivering right now. I have checked, he smokes Shivaji bidis too."

Four days went by, but Amrita's condition did not improve. Nawab and Ashika visited the hospitalregularly to see her. On one of their visits, they happened to meet S.I. Joglekar. He enquired about them and learned from the hospital staff that he was an ex-employee there, as well as Amrita's *rakhi*-brother,he had his own business of trading gold now and Ashika was his wife. Having learned all this, he ruled out their names from the list of suspects. Somehow, he was convinced that Dagdu was the culprit, but he wanted to gather more evidence before arresting him.

Nawab and Ashika were equally disturbed by Amrita's deteriorating medical condition and suggested Aadil to shift her to some other hospital for better treatment. "I will take care of all the medical expenses, you don't worry.She is my sister," Nawab told Aadil. Somehow, they convinced Aadil for it and he went to speak to Dr.Randhawa about it,however, Dr.Randhawa didn't allow it. Helpless, they remained mute spectators of Amrita's successively deteriorating condition.

Due to Nawab's increased engagement at the hospital during these tragic times, his business of gold smuggling suffered a considerable dent,while Salim seeked to take advantage of the situation and tried to mislead the syndicate involved in this gold smuggling business. He colluded with a rival group and struck a deal with them to eliminateNawab.By this time, Nawab had gained expertise in the entire operation of gold smuggling and had his own close confidantwho tipped him off about Salim's plan to eliminate him. Nawab discussed about the same with his confidant and decided to lay a trap forSalim.He spread the news that he would be visiting *Bada Kabristan*at Chandanwadialone to offer his prayers overBarkat Ali's grave on December 12th.

On receiving this information, Salim plannedhis operation for the same date, unaware that Nawab had already planned a counter operation against him.

At about 8 PM on 3rd December, Friday, Aadil walked out of the Haaji Ali dargaah after offering his prayers. He walkedover to the*kabutarkhana* and sat there watching the sunset. He got a bit emotional as he recollected sitting at the same place with Amrita very often before. She wasn't there with him that day, but her memories were. Aadil got drawn into another sequence of memories again. He remembered her in her blue sari, her long hair loose over her shoulders, a blue bindi on her forehead and deep love reflecting in her eyes.

"You shouldn't wear this blue sari," Aadil had said.

"Why?You don't like it?" teased Amrita.

"No, it's not that."

"Then?"

"Actually, you look very beautiful in this blue sari."

"Ohh, I see…"

"Why don't you understand?"

"Understand what, Aadil?"

"You see, I love you so much and when I see you in this blue sari, I feel like I am losing control over myself," confessed Aadil.

"What do you want?"

"Right now, I just want to kiss you," said Aadil and leaned in towards her to kiss her. She surrendered herself willingly in his arms.

Aadil further remembered them walking on the footpath next toHaaji Ali. It was night-time, a full moon was out and the sea was calm.

"I feels so good when you are here with me," Amrita had said."Me too. I hope these good times remain forever," said Aadil and kissed her again.They had continued to walk on together, hand in hand, till they reached a peanut seller and Aadil called out to him,"Give me some*mungfali*,please."

A peanut seller came up to him this day too and said, "Sir, do you want some *mungfali?* Take it, sir,sir, take it…" While he continued calling after Aadil, the latter noticed a familiar face of the cafe manager approaching him.

The manager handed the peanut vendor some cash and took a share of peanuts from him. It took Aadil a while to come out of his dazed semi-conscious state and register the presence of the cafe manager in front of him. He offered Aadil some peanuts which he hesitatingly took.

"How come you are here?"asked Aadil.

"I have been searching for you since the day I learned about Amrita madam. Who is that bastard? Just take care of yourself, everything will be fine.If you need any help, please do let me know. I knew I'd find you here because she used to tell me about you both, how you visitedSiddhivinayak onTuesdays and Haaji Ali on Fridays. I took a chance. You don’t worry, sir.She will recover.”

Aadilsmiled and breathed in a deep sigh. Both of them soon left since it was getting too late.

At 11:30 PM inDharavi,Dagdu Aandhale came out of his residence, feeling hesitant and nervous. He was carrying some bags which he was trying to conceal. He looked to his left, then right to make sure that no one was watching him. However, he was completely ignorant of the police constable who had been following him all day and sat hidden not very far away, keeping a strict eye on all his activities.

Dagdu got onto his bicycle and paddled it towards Bandra Khadi, but before reaching Khadi, the police constable caught up to him and recoveredhis bag from him.He was further taken into custody.

The police van which had him inside rushed towards the police station. The police constable yelled at him inside, "You bloody dog! Trying to run away from us?See how I beat you now."

Dagdu pleaded innocence, "Sir, please leave me. I haven't done anything."

"You haven't done anything?You rascal!" he exclaimed and started beating him.

"Sir,don't beat me, please," pleaded Dagdu.

"You motherfucker, do you even realize what you've done to that poor girl? What wrong did she do to you, bastard?" he yelled and continued to beat him.

Dagdu started shouting and requested the constable not to hit him anymore.

"You asshole, shut up.Just shut up. Wait and watch what my boss does to you in the morning, you rascal," he said and threw him in a locker.

The next morning, Dr. Wadia and Dr. Aadil discussed the matter of medical tests for Amrita, while Nafisa, Nawab and Ashika stoodby. Aadil couldn't stop his tears since Amrita hadn't recovered yet. "She is my fiancée, doctor.We were going to get married," he said while crying. All of them tried to comfort an inconsolable Aadil.

"Everything will be alright," said Dr.Wadia, while Nafisa, Nawab and Ashika simply continued to look at Aadil helplessly. Aadil read her medical report and screamedin agony. Nafisa took him in her arms and patted him gently. Nawab and Ashika tried to hide the tears in their eyes, but couldn't. Dr.Wadia felt great pain himself to witness all this.

At the police station, S.I. Jogalekar interogatedDagdu. He finally confessed his crime and revealed the entire story to him, specifically the reason why he had done such a thing with Amrita. Dagdu confessed that he felt specially attracted towards her, and her relationship with Aadil didn't go well with him. He couldn't take a Hindu brahmin girl marrying a Muslim man. He confessed to staring at her body a lot while cleaning or doing other jobs around the hospital.One afternoon, he had even seen Aadil kissing Amrita in her cabin. He had come on the pretext of taking some medical report, but when he entered her cabin and Amrita saw him, she left the file that she was studying and went close to him. The very next moment, they were both kissing each other, not aware that Dagdu was around.

"I was angry and couldn't control it," he confessed."She used to shout at me all the time for no reason at all. She never allowed me to drink, nor gave me money when I asked for it, so I decided to take revenge.That day, I learned through someone's conversation that Aadil was to leave early, and when I saw all of them leaving that evening, I decided to teach her a lesson and entered her cabin after her."

His entire confessional statement was recorded by the police officer and he was sent for a medical check up before being produced in court for remand.

That afternoon, inspector Jogalekar drove to the hospital. Upon entering, he headed straight for Dr. Randhawa's cabin and informed him about Dagdu's confession and arrest. He further enquired about the victim's condition and whether she would be able to give a statement against him in court. Dr.Randhawa answered in negative as Amrita hadn't recovered as yet and was in no position to give any statement.

"Doctor, identification of the accused by the victim is a must and her statement will only strengthen the case and bring justice to her," said S.I.Joglekar. Dr.Randhawa assured him of his complete co-operation.

In the evening of the same day, Dagdu was presented before the court and was sent to police custody for a week. In the meantime, Dr.Randhawa called up the Chairman of the trust and updated him on the proceedings. He instructed the doctor to co-operate with the police, but not at the cost of the hospital's reputation.Though they were being quite sympathetic towards Amrita,the hospital's reputation required to be guarded by them as well. Dr.Randhawa was intelligent enough to understand what job he had cut out for himself, and consequently planned tosabotage theprosecution's case. Dr.Wadia was not initially in agreement with this, but was later taken on board this sabotage plan.

Dagdu languished in police custody for two days,while Dr.Randhawa and Dr. Wadia held secret meetings with a high profile criminal lawyer at his Fort office, who designed all sorts of plans for them to grant the hospital a clean chit.

In a well designed plan, it was decided to plant a witness who could prove that Dagdu wasn't present in the hospital at the time of crime. This would confirm that though the crime happened inside the hospital, the culprit wasn't an employee of the establishment, but an outsider over which the hospital had no control, and therebycouldn't be blamed. In their selfish thinking, they forgot that they were denying justice to a woman who had been a part of their own institution for so long. After great research and effort, Dr.Randhawa came to know of Dagdu's friendship with Alok Rai from Dharavi and thepan shop were Dagdu and Alok used to meet. Dr.Randhawa met with Alok along with a lawyer and bought him over, asking him to cook up the theory that on the day of the incident, Dagdu had left forBhiwandi with him to satisfy his pleasures.They further bought the sex worker whom Dagdu had visited in Bhiwandi. In a tactic understanding with the lawyer, it was decided that he would arrange for a pro bono defence lawyer for Dagdu.Operation sabotage was carried out so secretively that nobody at the hospital was even made aware of the fact that Dagdu had been arrested.

On 10th December, Dagdu's remand was to be heard by the court, when the planted pro bono defence lawyer appeared and pleaded the court not to extend Dagdu's custody. It didn't take much time for S.I. Joglekar to understand the game played by the hospital's seniors, but he couldn't say much against them. Regardless, the court extended Dagdu's custody further by a week.

On 12th December at 9 AM, Nawab reached Bada Kabristhan at Chandanwadi to offer prayers at Barkat Ali's grave. The next moment, he saw six men in white kurta pyjama approaching him from the front, and one from behind. Nawab knew that this man was none other than Salim.

He signalledat one of his henchmen to shoot at Nawab. Nawab looked up where his own shooters had been waiting in advance. They had hid themselves in tree branches on the otherside where the Hindu cremation ground was, only a stone's throw from the Kabristhan.Before Salim's henchmen could fire at Nawab,an indiscriminate and silent firing from Nawab's henchmen made all of Salim's men and Salim himself drop down to the ground, dead, in only a fraction of seconds. Nawab's henchmen had used silencer guns which made them all the more lethal.Aburial spot had already been prepared for them in advance at the same Kabristhan, so all their bodies were thrown into the burial pitwhich were immediately filled in with mud and concrete. In another two hours, it seemed as if nothing out of place had happened there. From Chandanwadi'sBada Kabristhan, Nawab headed back for his housein Worli.

The next morning, Nawab met Aadil at the hospital. S.I. Jogalekar was there too for Amrita's statement, when they all learned about Dagdu's arrest. They felt shocked and surprised at the hospital's approach towards the matter. Amrita still lay unconscious, so Dr.Randhawa could not give S.I. Joglekar the permission to interrogate her, and he returned empty handed again.

Nawab and Aadil went to see Amrita in her room. Nawabstood at a distance whileAadilapproached her and started crying."Get well soon, Amrita. You have to plan our wedding soon. Pleaseget up. You can't leave us like this.Please, get up."

Nawab simply lookedat him with barely controlled emotions.

"Nawab, tell your sister to please get up.She can't leave me like this.Not before I die, at least," cried Aadil.

Nawab consoled him somehow and took him out of Amrita's room.

In a few minutes, both of them went to Dr.Randhawa's cabin and confronted him regarding the secrecy maintained around Dagdu's arrest.

"It's the hospital'spolicy," reasoned Dr.Randhawa. "And it is in Amrita's best interest too."

"How is that? Please tell us," questioned Nawab.

Aadil just stared at Dr.Randhawa,then lefthis cabin.Nawab followedhim out.

On 17th December, Dagdu was presented in court again after his 14th day remand got over. Hewas then forwarded to a 15 days' judicial custody by the court. Knowing well the intentions of the hospital, S.I Jogalekar collected all the evidence he could and prepared a charge sheet to file in the court.Dagdu was charged with offence u/s 307 and 377 of the IPC.His case was committed to Sessions Court and a trial commenced thereafter from 23rdJanuary, 1977. The same day, the then prime minister called for fresh general elections for March 1977, and issued the release of all political prisoners who had been arrested during the period of emergency.

Dagdu was still languishing in jail, but the trial of his case expedited. During the same period, press attention was more towards the general elections, and come March 1977, a new government led by Morarji Desai was installed at the Centre. It was considered a victory against the atrocities done during the emergency. With the installation of Morarji Desai's Janata Party, the government emergency officially came to an end.

Aadil and Nafisa diligently took care of Amrita, through she hadn't gained consciousness as yet. They were helpless,but left no stones unturned in making efforts for her and getting over the unfortunate incident themselves. They were even discharged from their other duties at the hospital for the sake of Amrita, though they didn't wish to continue there anymore after learningof the hospital's intention to sabotage the prosecutions case.Nafisa stood by Aadil unwaveringly during these difficult times.

Nawab had taken complete control of his business and made fortunes. Nawab and Ashika's toddler son had now grown a little and would accompany them once in while to the hospital.

Dagdu's trial had taken speed too. It was to be concluded and the judgement was to be delivered in the coming few months.

At the trial, Alok Rai and the*panwala* of Dharavi deposed and gave evidence that Dagdu had gone toBhiwandi with them for pleasureon that fateful night.The prostitute with whom they were regular also deposed in favour of Dagdu.No further eye witness who had seen Dagdu before or after the incident could be produced by prosecution. S.I. Joglekar, an upright and honest officer, tried to stitch the threads together to make a good case in order to deliver justice for Amrita, but was let down by the institution she worked for. On the basis of merely a wrapper of Shivaji bidi, the prosecution case could not be tilted in favour. Prosecution could neither prove rape nor sodomy for the lack of evidence. The wooden rod that Dagdu had pushed into Amrita's anus after the heinous crime wasn't seized by the police officials inadvertently, and it all went in favour of Dagdu.He was acquitted by the sessions court on the afternoon of 16th August 1977 from all charges, u/s 307 and 377 of the IPC.

With time, Amrita's case lost most of the press attention and Dagdu's acquittal wasn't noticed by anyone except for Nawab,Ashika, Aadil, Nafisa and a few other well-wishers. Amrita lay in a persistent vegetative state on her hospital bed. Dr.Randhawa and Dr. Wadia were relieved with Dagdu's acquittal as their plan of getting a clean chit for the hospital had worked. They had been successful in proving that no one from the hospital was responsible for the crime, and that the police authorities had falsely implicated an employee of the hospital for it.It was established by Dagdu's verdict that the police officials had not been able to trace the real culpritwho was not from the hospital,but perhaps an outsider.

It was raining outside the sessions court on the day of the verdict. Nawab and Ashika along with Aadil and Nafisa got into Nawab's car and drove to his residence at Worli. Nawab had bought this property with an additional apartment adjacent to it, and had converted it into a much bigger space now. He felt angry at the whole system, especially at the hospital and its approach.The rest of them remained quiet as Nawab got up and looked out the balcony. A few municipal corporation contractors were engaged in some road repair work outside. In one corner of the road, a huge tar boiler was placed with fire underneath it. As he glanced at it and pondered,an idea came up in his mind. It was almost 6PM in the evening by then.

"Was this man Dagdu from Dharavi?" he asked Aadil.

"Yes," he replied.

Nawab keep quiet for a while, then asked Aadil and Nafisa to relax and be comfortable whilehe finished some business assignment, promising to return in some time. Before leaving, he kissed his toddler son and asked Ashika to take care.

Nawab reached the radio club in another half an hour and satdown with his close confidant. He expressedhis desire to have Dagdu abducted from Dharavi and brought to him. His henchman readily agreed to it and Dagdu was abducted from his Dharavi residence the same night. He had been fast sleep when they came to get him, relieved about getting acquittal for a crime that he knew he had committed.

Dagdu was brought to Nawab at his Radio Club late in the night. He could not understand anything,but he knew that something was just not right. Nawab had arranged for a tar boiler inside the Radio Club and four gas cylinders were placed beneath it with the fire on. The boiler tank was full of tar and had reached its boiling point. Nawab asked one of his henchmen to undress Dagdu, tie his hands and legs and stuff cotton in his mouth.For the next few minutes, Dagdu stood in that condition, nude and tied up. Nawab got up,dragged Dagdu over to the boiling tank and pushed hisface close to the boiling tar.

Dagdu was scared for his life.He soon realized what was going to happen to him.He just looked at Nawab with terrified eyes beforeNawab pushed him head-first into the boiling tar container and burned him alive.They kept pushing till his body was completely immersed in it. Within the nextten minutes, Dagdu's entire body had melted. Not even his bones remained intact. He instructed his men to empty the tar at the same place next to his house were the road repair work was being carried out. His men obeyed and finished the job before sunrise.

When Nawab returned home post midnight, he found everybody fast sleep. Ashika asked him for dinner, but he said it was done and went to sleep.

The next morning, Nawab looked out his balcony while sipping tea and took a deep breath. He had breakfast with his wife Ashika,his son Asman,and Aadil and Nafisa before heading tothe hospital to see his beloved sister Amrita. As he stood next to her bed, he felt a compelling urge to tell her that the court mighthave let go of the culprit, but her brother hadn't.

For the next two months, Nawab and Ashika routinely visitedthe hospital for Amrita, where they alsocaught up with Aadil and Nafisa. Nobody knew what happened to Dagdu, except that he disappeared the same night after his acquittal and remained untraceable. Even in Dharavi his neighbour's does not know what happened to Dagdu. Even

Dr.Randhawa, Dr. Wadia, Aadil, Nafisa and S.I. Jogalekar had no clue of his whereabouts.Not even Ashika ever came to know what happened.

On 21st October, Friday, it was the day ofDussehra. Aadil went to spend some time at Shivajipark next to the beach. Aadil was walking alone on the damp sand, but somebody was close at his footsteps. When Aadil heard his name being called out, he turned around to find Nafisa there. She caught up to Aadil and they started walking together.

"How long will you wait for Amrita to recover?" asked Nafisa.

"Till she is completely recovered," said Aadil flatly.

"And God forbid, if she doesn't?"

"I don't know,perhaps she will get well soon."

"Aadil, both of us know that she isn't going to recover."

Tears leaked out of Aadil's eyes, "I know, but you tell me…what can I do?"

Nafisa held Aadil and consoled him,"Relax, things will be fine."

Aadil gathered himself and said, "She won't get well, but we need to support her.Will you be with me to support her and take care of her?"

Nafisa held Aadil's hand firmly and looked into his eyes. "If that is what you wish for…I am more than willing. Amrita was your fiancée, but she was my friend too. I often felt jealous of her that she had you in her life, but the irony now is that she is lying helpless in bed at the hospital. I have always loved her as my best buddy.It shouldn't have happened to her."

Aadilheld Nafisa's hand and they walked away together.

On 25th November the next month, Aadil and Nafisa got married before amarriage registrar. Nawab, Ashika and Pritha stood witness to there marriage. Amrita was still in coma. Aadil and Nafisa's marriage did not affect their attitude towards her. She continued to be taken care of by both of them. The hospital staff was supportive throughout too. Aadil still desperately hoped for Amrita to recover, but one day passed after the other and nothing changed. Every person who was aware of this incident was praying for Amrita's recovery, right from thecoffee shop manager to all of the hospital staff, each of whom took out the time to come see her now and then.

On 12th December, 1977, the day of Al Hijra - the Islamic New Year, Aadil and Nafisa arrived at the hospital in the morning.Nawab and Ashika were also visiting that day. Dr.Wadia and Dr. Randhawa collected them all in the latter's cabin and declared that Amrita is dead. All of them rushed to the ward where she lay, and found out that she was indeed dead.

Aadil cried profusely by her bed, so did Nafisa. Nawab entered the room and saw his beloved sister resting forever. After the initial official clearance, her body was taken out of the I.C.U. S.I. Jogalekar was also informed about Amrita's demise. Since she didn't have any relatives, her body was first handed over to the police. Aadil,Nafisa, Nawab and Ashika later organised her last rites and she was cremated as per the Hindu rites. Aadil, NawabandS.I. Jogalekar lit her pyre together at Shivaji Park. Her remains were immersed in the Ganges at Haridwar. All the rituals post Amrita's death were performed with the help of a Brahmin pandit by her fiancé and rakhi brother, bothMuslim.

While returning from Haridwar in the chilli December weather around Christmas, Aadil, Nafisa,Nawab,Ashika and their little son Asman stopped at a small *dhaba* by the highway to have tea. A radio was on at full volume at the *dhaba* for all the customer to hear. Some advertisement was going on at that time. Aadil suddenly started searching for something in his pockets and bags frantically. Nafisa understood what he was looking for and took out a ring from her purse to hand over to him.

"I removed it from Amrita's hand before the rituals commenced.I know it's the engagement ring that you gave her," she said.

While they had their tea and snacks, a song from Guru Dutt's classic 'Kagaj Ke Phool', starring the legendaryWahida Rehman and Guru Dutt himself, came on the radio. "*Waqt Ne Kiya Kya Hasin Sitam, Hum Rahe Na Hum, Tum Rahe Na Tum.*" The new year was about to begin in a few days,and all of them returned to Bombay to resume their respective occupations.

After Amrita's demise, Aadil and Nafisahad no inclination to continue working at the Verma Memorial Hospital.In mid 1978, theyleft the hospitalto start their own clinic at Matunga. Pritha left forLondon during this period and found herself a groom there. She got married and settled there itself. Nawab expanded his business even further and led a happy life with Ashika and his son Asman.Whenever he got the time, he met up with Aadil and Nafisa.

In the beginning of 1979, on 11th January, Aadil and Nafisa were blessed with a girl child. They named her

'Aafreen'. Nawab and Ashika came to bless her and graced the occasion of welcomingthe girl child into their lives.

As time passed, Nawab and Ashika decided to move out of the country and settle in Dubai. On 07th June, 1979, after celebrating their respective consecutive birthdays with all their friends in Bombay, they boardedtheir flight to Dubai. Aadil, Nafisa, Dr.Randhawa and Dr. Wadia had all come to celebrate and bid themfarewell before they left. Before leaving India, Nawab handed over the reserves ofBarkat's business to his close confidants who had stood by him over all these years.They distributed the fortune amongst themselves and moved out of Bombay to go back to their respective native places for a better living.

A few months later, JP (Jaiprakash Narayan) who had fought against the emergency, died on 8th October 1979 in Bombay, just a week beforeDussehra and Diwali. For Aadil and Nafisa, however,Dussehra/Diwali had no meaning anyway in the absence of Amrita,so they didn't celebrate it either. Regardless, the nation mourned the death of its beloved JP.

After 40 long years

In the year 2018, Nawab and Ashika returned to India with their grown up son, a daughter-in-law, aswell as a grandson. They settled back into theirold flat inWorli, which Aadil and Nafisa had been taking care of in their absence. They had remained in close contact over all this time, and were now well into their senior years.They finally met at long last after an interval of forty years at their Worli apartment.

Aadil and Nafisa had come alone since their daughter Aafreen was already married and had moved out of the country to settle in USA. They had no other child after Aafreen. Nawab's son, daughter-in-law and grandson had gone out for shopping. When Nawab enquired about the hospital, Aadil informed him that Dr. Jagmohan Randhawa had retired, Dr. Wadia was no more, while Dagdu Aandhale had still not been found, and nobody knew his whereabouts.

Nawab got up and looked out of his balcony.It was 8 PM in the evening."Worli has changed a lot in the last 40years. Bombay itself has taken on a new name, Mumbai,"said Aadil.

Nawab remained silent for a while, then replied, "Yes indeed, it has changed." He then called Aadil, Ashika andNafisa to step into the balcony. They all sensed something odd in his behaviour.

"You know, Nawab, Verma Memorial has redeveloped into ahuge hospital complex now. Even its name was changed by somehigh profile rich businessman from Mumbai," Aadil said.

Nawab still remainedsilent. Aadil,Nafisa and Ashika joined him in the balcony. "You guys want to know where Dagdu is?" asked Nawab.

"What!?" all of them exclaimed together. He pointed to the huge complex visible across the road and narrated to them the entire boiling tar episode. Next to the road where he had ordered his henchmen to deposit the tar, there now stood a huge complex. That particular part of the road was now covered by the building's gate. All of them were speechless, but had a spark in their eyes.

They all then returned to the dining room andwaited for Nawab's son and daughter-in-law to return. Aadil picked up a remote from the sofa and switched on the new branded TV which Nawab had bought upon his return to India. A popular contemporary news anchor came on and screamed, "The nation wants to know…"

Aadil switched off the TV immediately, andturned on the Radio FM on his mobile instead.An old song inMukesh's voice from the movie 'Mera Naam Joker' came on. "Jane Kaha Gaye Vo Din, Kehate The Teri Rah Me,Nazaro Ko Hum Bichaayenge. Chaahe Kahi Bhi Tum Raho,Chahenge Tumko Umra-bhar,Tum Ko Na Bhool Payenge."Nawab looked at Aadil, while Nafisa and Ashika just smiled.

After dinner, Aadil and Nafisa bid goodnight to Nawab and Ashika, and took their leave.Nawab and Ashika escorted themdown to the ground floor parking where Aadil and Nafisa's BMW X3 was parked. Before they got in the car, Ashika hugged Nafisa,while Aadil hugged Nawab.

"This will remain a secretbetween us and won't be shared with anyone," Aadil and Nafisa assuredNawab.

Nawab just smiled and looked into Ashika's eyes. "Let's not share it with our children either," he said. "At least,not before I die."

Aadil and Nafisa drove out of Worli, while Nawab and Ashika returnedto their home. Their son and daughter-in-law returned after sometime and headed straight for their room with their son. Nawab was standing quietlyin the balcony. "The children have returned, Nawab.It has gotten late. Come, let's sleep," said Ashika. Nawab turnedto look intoher eyes and nodded.

The next morning, Bombay…no, Mumbai was full of life as usual.

9 789388 333542

Printed by Libri Plureos GmbH in Hamburg, Germany